The Reunion

PROLOGUE

Her heart pounded in her ears. Thin-edged branches tore against her skin as she sped through the overgrown woods. Sweat and tears poured down her face. The pain was almost beyond bearing. Every inch of her body ached.

Who was he? Heavy steps and rustling leaves told her he was close behind. A searing pain in her shin caused her to fall on her face. She turned over and attempted to get up.

It was too late. An arm reached out and yanked her to him.

With her arms pinned over her head, her legs were locked under him. In one swift move, he unfastened his belt and secured it around her wrists so his hands were free. Free to grope, free to rip at her. He pushed her shirt up. Ripped off her bra. Rough hands rubbed her sore, swollen breasts. Then he sank his teeth into her left breast. Hard. She had dirt caked in her eyes, and combined with sweat and tears and shock, her vision was scarce at best. He was just a blur on top of her. Everything was fuzzy, but there was red, something very red. Somewhere there was blood. The pain ripped through her again, as he penetrated her over and over. The dryness inside made it all the more painful. Then, without warning, he slung her over and entered her from her backside as she squirmed and fought beneath him to no avail. He used one hand to keep her restrained, and the other was tangled in her hair. Bile rose to the back of her throat. The acrid smell of stale cigarette smoke lingered around him and made her gag.

"Oh, God, no, please help me!" she screamed, almost shrieking, in between a stream of tears.

"Help me, I beg someone, help me, make it stop!" she screamed.

I'm going to die! I want to just curl up and die, anything to make it stop.

Trying to forget the pain, she fiercely gulped for air, in and out, in and out as he pummeled into her tiny frame. When will he be satisfied? How many times had she broken free only to be caught and the horror repeated? Three, or was it four? Her nails dug into the ground and gripped the earth for security, for support, anything at all that would help ease the excruciating nightmare. She closed her eyes, praying, trying to have faith, all the while feeling his thick, loud breath on her back, causing acid to churn in her belly. She felt drained, hollow, and lifeless. With her eyes still closed, she never saw the blow to the head coming. She suddenly saw double. Haziness. Everything became dark and faint, and then she was out cold. Lying still. Too still in the damp mosquito-infested bed of debris.

Her consciousness slipping away, the fear was still there. Her last thoughts before she lost consciousness were: I must live.

CHAPTER 1

If she didn't go soon, she may change her mind.

"Suzanne, can you please hurry with those Talman figures? I was supposed to be on my way to Ohio an hour ago," Jamie said.

She half-anticipated, half-dreaded the trip. Ten years was a long time to be away.

"They're under the pile on your right. No, the other pile on your right," Suzanne instructed as Jamie grabbed the wrong stack. "The numbers are more lucrative than we projected. It should be another hefty profit." Suzanne paused to look at Jamie's paper-strewn desk. "You know, I could organize that mess for you while you're gone."

"Absolutely not, don't touch anything. I have a system," Jamie said.

"Why are you going home for the reunion anyway? You've been nothing but distracted, moody, and frankly, a royal pain in the ass since you announced you were going."

"I haven't been moody, thank you. I'm just nervous. I haven't been home in over ten years. I have a right to be a little jittery." Especially about facing the life she'd left behind. Jamie wasn't even sure why she'd agreed to the trip. Part of it was guilt. She had consistently given her friends excuses over the years, stalling the inevitable.

"What, old boyfriends?" Suzanne asked.

"No, my two best girlfriends since we were three years old," Jamie said. A sudden pang of nostalgia ripped through her heart. The truth was, she missed her friends and conversations that didn't relate to work. Work was her life.

Jamie climbed from young ad executive up to the Chief Marketing Director for Jordan Marketing Strategies. She held the record for bringing in failing businesses: marketing each one with her unique touch and saving them from bankruptcy by educating them on their market and teaching them how to gain clients. Her work consumed her. It kept her focused and her life on a routine just as she liked it.

Henry poked his head in her office.

"Hi, Henry. Can I help you with something?" Jamie asked. Henry had worked for the firm for two months now.

He shook his head. "Actually, I thought I could help you finish up any work so you can finally take that vacation that everyone claims you refuse every year."

In five years, Jamie had never missed a day, not one. Jamie resigned herself to accepting the help, wishing she could finish in solitude, but knowing the others could do the work.

"Fine. I'm out of here. You can team up with Suzanne on these accounts. I'll check in occasionally, and you can call my cell if you have questions. I'll see you in four weeks."

*   *   *

Jamie looked around at her surroundings before entering the security code that led into her flat located in downtown Chicago. She knew she was being paranoid, but she had good reason to be, considering her experience ten years ago.

She looked at the trendy building and wondered, yet again, why she needed such a luxury when she was never there. Most of the spacious rooms were often unused, serving as little more than a sign of her hard work and long hours. Pricey picture frames, large vases, and antique furniture were supposed to personalize the rooms, though she hadn't seen the point of that either. But a small reputable interior design company had been one of her first clients, and the nice husband and wife duo decorated the flat for her.

It was her first success story. After rescuing their firm, Jamie had allowed the couple to try their hand at her empty rooms. The outcome was a modern look with a touch of glamour. It was somewhat of a shame how rarely anyone saw it. More often than not, she would fall asleep at the office, change, shower, and get back to work. "But hey, I can afford it, so why not?"

Her life suited her well. Yet lately, hints of loneliness clouded her busy days. It was time for the trip.

She wasn't even sure what to pack. Most of her wardrobe was for her work, which didn't seem appropriate clothing for her hometown. Even her tailored navy blue suit she was wearing looked unsuitable.

She gathered all the essentials and what outdoor clothing she had and shoved it into her overstuffed suitcase. She packed her headphones and tossed in a few CDs. When everything else was wrong, she could always lose herself in music.

She glanced at her watch. The taxi wasn't due for several more minutes. She snatched a Diet Pepsi out of the fridge and popped it open. Scouring the cupboards, she found a couple small bags of salt and vinegar chips nestled next to some cans of peas that had probably been bought by her housekeeper when she first moved in. Her housekeeper had long since given up on stocking the kitchen with healthy foods, and now gave in to Jamie's liking of junk. The chips would do for now. Maybe on the way she could stop at McDonald's, she thought, as always feeling lucky for her high metabolism. Other than the occasional jog in the park or a swim, she didn't have time to exercise.

With snacks in hand, she moved out on to her balcony. This was one of her favorite spots. She turned her face to the sun. The warm day was clear, and she could see out to the lake where the top of the Ferris wheel at Navy Pier poked above the building. The busy streets below, overcrowded with both people and vehicles, were comfortably familiar, but so different than the long open roads back home.

She certainly had come a long way since her days at Ball State University. Two months into college, her parents had died in a plane crash on the way back from Australia. They'd saved for over five years to afford her mom's dream vacation. Four weeks of sightseeing in Sydney. The emptiness of it all shot instantly to the pit of her stomach as she allowed old memories to resurface. So many things she never got to tell them. Instinctively she reached for the only piece of jewelry she wore. Her parents sent the onyx necklace as a gift the first week they were there. She never took it off, for it seemed as long as she wore the necklace, they were there with her. Being the only child, they were all she'd ever had. Of course, Alex and Samantha, her two best friends, had always been there for her, but at the time of her parents' death they were off

finding their own way in life.

The intercom rang, pulling Jamie back to the present. She

headed inside, grabbed her bags, and with a deep breath, walked out

the door.

*   *   *

Samantha Connors jumped off her boat and threw the ropes

up on the deck. As she worked, a pack of locals tripped over each

other, offering their assistance to secure her lines. She created quite

a stir, as usual. She then skillfully backed in her thirty-two-foot Sea

Ray, her baby "Knot His" into her slip. She couldn't help but smirk

every time she glanced at the name "Knot His." At least she got

something out of the son of a bitch. No one abused Sam Connors

and got away with it. She grabbed a bunch of plastic snakes she'd

bought at the dollar store and tossed them around the boat. That

should keep the damn birds from shitting all over her boat, at least

for a week or two.

She swept up her thick, tangled mass of jet-black hair and

clipped it above her head. In doing so, she showed off more than a

glimpse of her toned figure outfitted in her usual fishing attire, a tight cut-off tee, very short cut-off Levis, and a pair of sandals. The ensemble blended well against her sunbathed skin and made her tattoo of a fire-breathing dragon on her lower left calf more noticeable.

Sam finished securing her vessel and, with an hour to spare, headed for the outdoor bar located at the north end of the marina. She couldn't help but smile at the contrast to her previous life of hotel rooms, smoky bars, and cons. Hers was a quiet existence now. Miles upon miles of water served as her backyard. No crowded bars, drunken fights, late nights, or stolen memories. There was nothing better than the comfort of her boat and the rock of the waves lulling her to sleep.

She chose a spot at the bar. "A shot of Jack and whatever's on draft, please. I'll also try one of those perch sandwiches with extra tartar sauce that I've been hearing everyone brag about," Sam said.

If the sandwich was half as good as the smell, she'd be impressed. Sam enjoyed the comfortable surroundings of the small tavern. Stuffed fish and sporting equipment splashed against the walls captured the character of the town. She'd stopped in a few times, but never had a chance to try the locally famed fish.

Sam's thoughts were interrupted by the usual gossip from the table full of men directly behind her.

"What's a woman like that doing alone with a boat that size? Where's her husband?" asked one guy.

His buddy next to him said, "According to a local captain, she comes in here a few times every year. She lives alone on the boat, traveling around all year making stops a few weeks at a time here and there. Rumor has it, the boat was her husband's before she killed him."

Samantha let out a soft laugh. That was certainly a new twist to her much talked about past. It didn't seem a woman could do her own thing without something being wrong with her. Gossip never bothered her, though. Usually, it meant people had nothing better to do. She finished her beer and sandwich and headed toward the door. But before she walked out, she couldn't resist a little fun. She stopped in front of the table.

"Don't worry, he didn't feel a thing. He was sleeping when I did it," she said with the conviction that was part of her character.

Satisfied with herself, she strolled out the door, leaving her gossipers in stunned silence. She was looking forward to how that would develop by the time she got back. Damn old timers thought a woman couldn't do anything unless a man was along.

*   *   *

Alex painstakingly tucked, dusted, swept, and polished her old brick farmhouse. She started in the bedroom, which was decorated simply in farm antiques, old milk jugs, and signs. Clean, crisp white sheets were on each bed. She'd even gone to the trouble of picking bunches of wildflowers out of the backyard and displaying them in old Pepsi bottles throughout the house.

The bathrooms adjoining each bedroom were old and in desperate need of repair. But even if shabby, they were both sparkling fresh and clean. The oversized refrigerator was stocked full of various meats, fresh fruits, and vegetables for the first time in years. The terrace doors adjoining the family room were open, allowing the fresh scent of country air to drift in, and the warm summer sun to warm the rugs.

There was no color coordination or design pattern involved in the decor, but a comfortable mix of items she had picked up here and there—combined with what her parents had left—filled her home. The final result was one of love and family.

She was nervous. After all, she was the only one who had stayed in Ohio while they went off to Chicago and Michigan. When they had been off closing deals and seeing America, she had been showing horses at the county fair.

She changed into a clean Ohio State T-shirt and overalls and brushed through her long cinnamon-colored hair, securing it back into her standard braid. With it off of her face, her skin glowed and drew out her high cheekbones.

She headed downstairs and out to tend to the animals.

*   *   *

Doug pounded the nail with more muscle than he probably needed. His thoughts weren't on the nail or the door he was attempting to fix. He thought if he kept himself busy his mind wouldn't wander. He was wrong.

Unable to sleep, he had been making attempts at keeping busy for hours. He grabbed a deli sandwich and a soda out of his

cooler and gave into his wandering thoughts as he made a feeble
attempt at lunch.

No matter how hard he tried to pretend that today was a
normal day, he knew it wasn't. He reasoned that it wouldn't affect
him. Sure, he'd run into her. It'd be hard not to in such a small
town. He was an adult. He would say hello and be civil. But, if that
were the case, why was his heart thumping madly?

He didn't want the news of her return to bother him, but his
mind raced onward. He often wondered if he ever entered Jamie's
thoughts. His own memories of her were clear. How would he feel
when he saw her again? What the hell happened all those years ago?
His head was pounding from the stress he was placing on himself
with all these unanswered questions.   When Alex broke the
news to him that Jamie was coming home, he had merely stared at
her, tongue-tied. For the first time in ten years, he would be face to
face with the woman who had broken his heart.

CHAPTER 2

Jared paced impatiently at the bus station waiting for Jamie and Sam. How the hell did he allow his sister to con him into this anyway? With all the work he had to do, he didn't have time to spend half a day driving into town and waiting for two females. He wished they would hurry the hell up. After all, the hay wasn't going to bale itself, now was it?

Why the hell couldn't Alex do this herself?

He heard a familiar voice and turned around. And there she was, still drop-dead gorgeous. Samantha hadn't changed a bit.

"How's it hanging, handsome?" Sam yelled across the station. For a long moment she looked back at him. Alex's older brother was still as handsome as ever with those small, dark curls springing casually along his forehead. One look at his muscular build told her he was still running his family's farm.

She thought back to her high school fling with him. She had been a sophomore, Jared a senior, when he had taken her to the Winterball. She had lost her virginity that night in the hayloft in his parents' barn. He was gentle and caring, and they had dated for a few months. Too bad he wasn't her type—a little too conservative and set in his ways for her tastes. Tending to a field and farm all day, stuck in this town her whole life, was not on her agenda.

"Hi, Sam. You look great, as always," Jared said in a deep voice. "Let's get these loaded in the pickup, and we'll have a drink across the street while we wait for Jamie."

"Sounds good, but not until I get a hug," she said, pulling him towards her.

*   *   *

Three hours and two beers later, Jared was catching Sam up on local gossip.

"Remember Doug Miller, Jamie's guy in high school. Well, he married Amy Mathews after she got pregnant. Then she ran off a couple of years ago with a truck driver. Took her clothes, left a note and everything else behind, including her now four-year-old daughter, Haley."

"No shit. How'd he handle it?" Sam asked.

"Not too bad, I don't think. He was never really in love with her. He tried to make it work for his daughter's sake."

"Did he ever remarry?"

"No, he never got over Jamie."

"I thought I'd find you two in here."

Sam turned around in her bar stool and saw Jamie standing there in a pair of Levis, with a hole in the right knee and tear in the left pocket. Completing the ensemble was a faded concert t-shirt and pair of old but clean Reeboks.

"I thought you had a job out there in Chicago. You think they could afford to get you some clothes," Jared said.

"I do have clothes, lots of them, and a job, thank you, but nothing quite suitable for wallowing out on the farm in cow shit. So I dug these out of the closet."

"I can see the first item on our list will be shopping," said Samantha.

"Come on, let's go. If I don't get you both out to the farm soon, Alex will never let me hear the end of it," Jared said, grabbing Jamie's gear.

"Nice to see you, too," Jamie said. Following him to the truck, she decided he was still as bossy as before.

They drove away from the small city and onto a long, narrow dirt path. Jamie couldn't believe how much everything looked as it did ten years ago. Other than a new video store, a car wash, and a few houses, everything was pretty much the same. She did notice the upgrade on the local post office. The trailer had been traded in for a one-story brick building, complete with a huge sign out front. Once they hit the country though, for as far as she could see, were rows of corn and wide-open land. No tall buildings or busy streets filled with noise. The tallest structure she could see was the water tower. Looking toward the sky, she saw birds soaring amongst the clouds and the sun beginning its drop for the day, creating a purplish and orange hue as background. The atmosphere alone gave her a calm she hadn't experienced in a while. Maybe this was exactly what she needed. A little rest and relaxation. Her apprehension about this trip was probably for nothing.

*   *   *

Alex came barreling down the porch steps. She caught her foot on a loose board, causing her to lose her balance, and slid into the rail. Smiling despite the spill, she decided to wait for them to get to her.

Jamie laughed. "Still as clumsy as ever, I see. Come here and give me a hug," she said, drawing Alex in close to her. The girls took turns welcoming each other.

"I missed you both, it's been too long," Alex said.

"All right, that's enough," Jared stated as they drew him in for a group hug. "I'm gonna need a beer," he said.

"Let's go out to the porch. You two can relax and bring me up to date," Alex said.

Alex assigned Jared the task of taking up the girls' suitcases while they went to relax and catch up on gossip out on the front porch.

Jared sulked as he trudged up and down the stairs several times unloading the luggage.

"You'd think they were moving in permanently with all this crap. First chauffeur, now a damn bellhop. What next?" he murmured.

He needed an escape for a little while before they put him to work again. At least that was what he told himself as he glanced out the window at Samantha's long, sexy legs propped up on the picnic table. She was slouched back in a lawn chair and looked extremely comfortable.

"I'm going into town to grab a couple pizzas for dinner. Triple cheese, pepperoni, and sausage, right?"

"Right!" they yelled back in unison.

Jared headed out the drive in his Ford pick-up. He knew the next four weeks were going to be very long. He also knew he'd require more than a few cold showers along the way.

*   *   *

"So, how're your parents doing, Alex?" Jamie asked.

"Loving Fort Lauderdale. They've been there for five, almost six years now, and love every minute of it. With just Jared and me left, I handle the animals, and Jared tends to the farming. I finally convinced him to have a few kids from the high school give us a hand for the summer. Keeps us busy. But enough about me, how are you both? Sam, are you still living on that boat?"

"You bet."

"How's that ex-husband of yours? Giving you any problems?" Alex asked.

"No, last I heard he was in jail somewhere over in Columbus for beating on some woman. That asshole still can't keep his hands to himself."

Jamie rolled her eyes, "I never did like the guy. I told you he was trouble from the day he walked into school. I could see it in his eyes, always spoiling for a fight."

"That's what interested me at the time. I was young and rebellious. It was fun as his accomplice. Helping him hustle innocent bystanders on a pool table, causing trouble. Once he started using me as a punching bag, it was time to move on. How about you, Jamie? Any new loves?"

"Just my work and an occasional dinner date here and there. No time or interest for anything serious."

Sam turned to Alex.

"I like what you've done with the place. You better watch it, if I get too comfortable I may never leave," Sam joked.

"That wouldn't be so bad," Alex said.

"You're stuck with us for four weeks," Jamie said. "We'll see if you still think so then. I bet Jared's not too thrilled having to share his space with two extra women."

"Oh, he loves it as much as I do. He just has to grumble so it doesn't show. No offense, Jamie, but I'm sure he really likes having Sam around," Alex teased.

"Oh, yeah, like he's pining over some girl he had sex with in high school. His little sister's friend who drove him nuts," Sam said, laughing.

"Shh. Don't move. Look," Jamie said.

"What?" Sam said.

"A butterfly," Jamie said. She was mesmerized by the exquisite orange and brown creature peacefully perched on the armrest of her chair. She was surprised at how beautiful a butterfly could be and how serene the presence of one could make her feel.

"Very good, I take it they don't have those in the city," Sam said.

"Never mind," Jamie said as the insect gently took flight. "So, what's there to do in this town?" she asked.

"Same things when you left, enjoying the nice country air," Alex said.

Jamie rolled her eyes. "Great."

"Actually, we have a full schedule. There's the festival, the clambake, and, of course, the reunion. I figure we could do some shopping, and I'm sure Jared has some ideas of his own. Never known him not to put the guests to work," Alex said.

"I can't wait. It's a much-needed change of pace," Sam said. "Right, Jamie?"

Jamie tried to keep focused on the conversation. But all of a sudden, she had an uneasy feeling she was being watched. "What? Sorry."

A prickly feeling ran through her, and a cold knot formed in her stomach. It was probably just a curious animal of some sorts. It'd been a long time since she'd been in the country.

CHAPTER 3

The woman of his dreams, his first and only love, had come
home to him. She was meant to be his and his she would be. He
could be a patient man. He'd proven that already. She had given
him time to plot his next move. He knew she would come home
eventually. And now that she was here, it was time for her to accept
her fate.

She slipped away once, ten years ago. Leaving him alone. No good-byes. No note. No visit. Nothing. She just packed up and left. He missed her. Ached for her. Needed her. Now he would have her. He could still remember the feel of her skin, the beauty of it, and it made him moan softly. Of course she would have to pay for leaving him. That couldn't go unnoticed. The bitch broke his heart and left it empty. For that, she would need to be punished. Women needed to know their place. His uncle had taught him that years ago.

He noticed a couple of vehicles pulling up the drive and decided he'd been here long enough. It was too early in his plan to be taking any chances. His plan was too important to be altered. With a twinge of disappointment, he packed away the binoculars and headed out the back end of the farm, which led to a clearing. Soon Jamie would be with him. Very soon.

CHAPTER 4

The girls were lazily bathing in the scorching sun, flipping

idly through beauty magazines, when two pickups pulled in the

drive. At the sound of slamming doors, Jamie saw Remy, the family

retriever, shoot from out of the ditch behind the river. He trotted

around to the driveway to greet the new arrivals, his light coat covered in mud. The dog howled his approval when he spotted his

master.

"Hey there, boy. The girls driving you crazy, too?" Jared

said as Remy rolled over on his back to get his tummy rubbed. His

tail flopped loudly on the ground when Jared honored his request.

Doug followed behind him, carrying a couple boxes of pizza

and a case of Coors Lite.

"Just remember, Doug, I warned you ahead of time," Jared

said as Doug chuckled and followed him around the side to the

porch.

The aroma of grease had the girls stirring to attention, and

they immediately sprang into action.

In one organized move, Sam grabbed the beer cans and

tossed them around to everyone. Alex pulled apart pieces of pizza,

set them on napkins, and dispensed them. Jamie, on the other hand,

sat still. She was shocked by the man who stood in front of her.

His compelling blue eyes, the firm features, the confident set

of his shoulders could lull any girl in a trance. Doug gave her a

smile that set her pulse racing. His grin was irresistible. The same

smile she so clearly remembered. It was as if she'd just seen him yesterday. That intense smile could still take her breath away if she let it. But, she wouldn't.

"Well, after ten years, you think a man could get a little more enthusiasm than that," Doug said, as he reached out his hands, motioning her over for a friendly embrace.

Jamie flushed. "Sorry, it's been a long time. You just caught me a little off guard," she said. Then she allowed Doug to pull her in for a hug. His arms around her sent happy shivers up her spine.

Doug tightened his arms around Jamie. Her sweet smell of jasmine, combined with the feel of her soft skin, still stirred something deep in him. He forced himself to pull away and took a long friendly look at her. Standing there in a bikini top, gym shorts, and bare feet, she looked as sensuous as she did ten years ago.

"It looks like the big city's been treating you good."

"I get by well enough," Jamie assured him as Sam handed Doug a beer.

"Have a seat, handsome, and tell me more about how you've been," Sam said.

"Hi, Sam, you look great as usual." Doug gave Sam a kiss on the cheek and helped himself to a patio chair. "Jared stopped by my house and said he needed some help entertaining some gorgeous women, and I couldn't refuse. Besides, I needed a break from work."

"That's not exactly how I phrased it, but the point's the same. Doug bought the old Carter place last year and is in the process of fixing it up," explained Jared. "Doing a decent job, too. Sure needed a lot of work."

"I got a good deal on it, and it keeps me busy. Alex has been helping me with the interior design. Had to get a pool in, too, so Haley would leave me alone," Doug said.

"Doug turned the garage into a workshop," Alex said. "He fixes and repairs just about anything." Alex turned to Doug. "Actually, Doug, I was going to see if you had the time and could work on the sink in the spare bathroom?"

"Just leave a list on the table."

"Don't forget the loose board on the porch before Alex breaks her neck," Jared added.

"I'll make sure that's first on the list."

"Thanks, I appreciate it." Alex gave Jared a nasty glare.

"Don't worry, Doug, we'll be out of your way." She surveyed Jamie's faded and torn jeans. "We're going shopping for the reunion."

Jamie looked back at her with wide eyes.

"Shopping. Ugh. What on earth for? I brought clothes," Jamie said.

"Mm-hmm. We see the clothes you brought," Samantha put in.

Alex laughed.

"Alex and I already decided we're going shopping," Sam said.

"I can't wait. There's a creek right here, and I'm going to spend the day in some mall looking for clothes I may wear once," Jamie said.

Alex caught the wry complaint in her voice and smiled at her friend.

"Oh, relax, we'll leave early and have plenty of time to sunbathe," she studied Jamie in amusement. "I see nothing's changed there."

Jamie shook her head.

The conversation turned from shopping as Doug spoke.

"Sam, what's this I hear about you living on a yacht, traveling around causing havoc with all the old fishermen?"

"I wouldn't exactly call it a yacht. I usually have about six months good weather, then I have to rent something for the winter. I'd like to buy something this year, maybe a cottage."

"You could get something here. The Taylor cottage is for sale. It would be fun, we could spend half the year together," Alex said.

"You never know." Sam raised her eyebrows at the possibility.

"How about you, Jared? I expected a ring on your finger by now," Jamie asked.

"Who has time to find a wife when I have Alex here as a slave driver?"

"Don't let him fool you. You can't kick him out of here. Jackie Myers has been trying to get his attention for a few years, but Jared has his heart set on his true love out there somewhere."

"My heart's been snatched by Haley Marie," he said and motioned Doug to show a picture of Jared's godchild.

Doug obliged with pure pride, passing around a portrait. The angelic child had a mass of bouncing golden locks and a pair of mesmerizing blue eyes that drew one in.

"She's adorable," admired Jamie.

"I think so, too, thank you," Doug said. "I'm blessed to have her. I'd like for you and Sam to meet her when she gets home. Grandpa and Grandma carted her off for a few weeks to the lake. How could I beat out swimming, Cedar Point, and Sea World?" he chuckled. "Speaking of which, I need to head home. Haley's calling before she goes to bed. See everyone tomorrow."

"I'll need your help entertaining again tomorrow evening," Jared said. "I was thinking we could cut some of that wood behind the barn for a fire, grill some steaks, and take a swim in the creek," Jared said.

"Count me in," Doug said as he climbed into his truck.

Doug drove home trying to keep his mind on the road, but it wasn't easy. Damn that Jamie!

He smiled, thinking back to the days when Jamie, Alex, and Sam would follow him and Jared around. Hanging out in the boys-only clubhouse, they would pretend the girls were a nuisance, telling them to quit pestering them. She was always there, ever since he could remember. At school, parties, school events, the clubhouse, the creek, each other's houses. They experienced all their firsts together. First dance. First kiss. First girl he held hands with, first girl he had dated. First love.

Of course, there was the night after the town festival. A single kiss he would never forget. Then, a week later, she was gone. No note, no calls, no explanations. He finally persuaded her parents to tell him. She had run off to Ball State. She hadn't even planned on going there.

No one would tell him why. He still didn't know.

After ten years and everything that had happened in both their lives, how the hell could a few hours rekindle so much sentiment? That single thought froze in his brain.

                              *   *   *

Jamie lay in bed, exhausted, unable to sleep. Mixed emotions were stirring inside her. Her friends had been great about respecting her privacy. Still, wouldn't they want answers? All they knew is she left home and got married. Todd Jenkins III came along, right at a time her heart was at its weakest. A controlling journalist, Todd was also a student at Ball State. He'd courted her, supported her when her parents died a week after getting to school, and taken her in, giving her security again. One month later, they were married; five months later, divorced. The problem with Todd was he also took in everyone else. He had come from money, and his parents had rented him a large colonial seven-bedroom house. Todd's only goal was to rebel against them and that he did. The house was constantly full of clouds of marijuana and naked students of both genders. Jamie went along with his ways, though never participating. But when he'd insisted she join him in one of his sexual escapades with five other students, she'd packed her bags.

She never looked back. She centered all her strength and energy into being a success. And success for her was graduating at the top of her class, earning two degrees, one in marketing and one in business. Funny, how it all fell into place. Business was never her intentions. Her original plans, she remembered, had been two years of dental school.

But, there was no dentist program at Ball State. And only a few classes were available, a few pertaining to marketing, since she hadn't planned on leaving town and didn't register ahead of time.

Through an internship, she found she was good at sales and could make decent money without a lot of hours. From there she was hooked.

After graduation, Jamie was immediately contacted by Jim Jordan of Jordan Marketing and offered an entry level position, which had been a godsend! She loaded up and moved to Chicago. Instantly pouring herself full force into her work, Jamie dedicated long hours night and day bringing in failing businesses. She created a whole new division for Jordan, and it landed her the top role as director.

The thought of what was to come tore at her insides and a wave of apprehension swept through her. She had to face this town, face old ghosts, remember everything, and put it to rest. And, God, seeing Doug again tugged at her heart. Though she always had feelings for Doug, she hadn't expected them to still be there. She wouldn't be sleeping any time soon.

She walked out to the porch and sat on the porch swing. The full moon danced brightly. The night air chilled and provided a slight breeze. She forgot how peaceful a quiet country night could be. She leaned back and breathed. This was better relaxation than any day spa. Her mind wandered back to Doug. Her heart swelled

with a feeling she had thought long since dead.

Then Jamie looked around, making herself aware of her

present surroundings again. Something didn't feel right. She had

goose bumps on her arms, and she was trembling. It was as if

something or someone was watching her. She felt sick. She stood

up quickly, scanning the woods and the creek from the porch. She

saw nothing but couldn't shake her uneasiness. Overcome with

terror, she ran back inside and locked every door in the house before

slipping back into bed to a fitful sleep.

CHAPTER 5

What a pleasant evening. Twice he got to see his sweetheart.
There she was, lounging on the porch, inviting him to join her. He
knew it was a risk to be back here again. He couldn't help himself.
A man had his limits. He was sure to be careful and keep a safe
distance between them. He couldn't take the chance of being
spotted. It would ruin everything.

He deserved this. Just one extra indulgence before his plan would begin to go into place. She got him so excited. He could feel himself go hard. No one could do that to him but Jamie. Sure, there were a few women throughout the years. Whores. All of them. Finally, he'd given up. They couldn't stir him like she did. It was best to save himself for her. To let his love build. He had plenty of time to plan for perfection. It was all figured out. She would be his wife and bear his children. She would resist at first, but she'd see. He would be patient and loving. She would learn to see she could depend on him.

They were meant for each other. It was their destiny. She would see all she would ever need was him. He would make sure of it. She'd come back, hadn't she? That was proof in itself. He was so aroused. He watched her, and he pleasured himself, closing his eyes and thinking soon she would be there doing it for him next time.

*   *   *

"I absolutely refuse to wear that thing. I might as well be naked!" Jamie complained.

"Just try it on. No one's asking for a lifelong commitment. Just walk in there and put it on," Sam ordered.

"Fine. If it means we can get out of this store, I'll try it on."

Jamie tried on the blue silk tank dress and walked out. The dress clung to her petite body, showing off just enough skin.

"Wow," Alex said. She whistled her approval.

Both Sam and Jamie glanced over at Alex, surprisingly shocked. She was after all usually the shy one, and in one loud gesture, she had the whole store gaping in their direction.

"What's gotten into you?" Sam asked.

"I'm evolving. And there's more where that came from."

"Wonderful. Now can we go?" Jamie asked.

They paid for their clothes and made their way across the street to the local tavern for lunch.

"The place hasn't changed a bit," Jamie said, looking around the tavern. Brown walls covered with beer paraphernalia. A variety of games to the left. Tables to the right. "I remember when we'd ride our bikes down here for lunch and play video games."

"Yeah, only now we don't have to drink milk with it," Sam smiled.

"You up for a challenging game of Ms. Pac Man?" Jamie asked the girls.

"Sure, why not, I love that game," Sam said.

"After that we need to make one more stop. I promised Jared while we're in town we'd go to the market and pick up some supplies for tonight's cookout," Alex said.

"Speaking of the cookout, I saw the way you and Doug looked at each other yesterday," Sam said.

"First of all, what the hell does shopping for a cookout have to do with Doug?" Jamie said. "Second of all, we didn't look at each other in any certain way. What you saw in my eyes was shock. That's all."

"Uh-huh," Sam said.

"For heaven's sake, that was ten years ago."

"I agree with Sam. There was a sparkle between…" Alex started.

"Whatever," Jamie interrupted. "Are we going to the store or what?"

She wasn't going to admit the instant rush of fervor at seeing him or the sudden jolt when he touched her. If she didn't admit it, it didn't happen.

                    *   *   *

Jared jumped off his tractor, satisfied with the day's work. A couple of kids from town were helping him for a few weeks while they had guests. He grabbed two beers out of the fridge and went to annoy Doug while he worked on the porch.

"Hey, I'll take one of those, thanks," Doug said, grabbing a beer.

"If you came to help, I'm pretty much finished for the day. I need to order some parts for the door and some new screen before I go any further."

"No, I just wanted to see about getting that wood ready for the bonfire tonight."

Doug tensed just thinking about seeing Jamie again. He pushed the thought of her aside and nodded. "Okay, let's go."

Doug and Jared were finishing up preparations when they heard Remy going nuts in the front yard—the girls were back.

"We could use some help up here," Sam called out. Remy raced to the backyard to lead them to the car.

Everyone worked together, carrying in groceries, unloading packages, and preparing dishes.

When the smell of cooked meat began wafting in the kitchen an hour later, the girls were ready to eat.

"Are those steaks done yet?" Alex called. "We're starving."

"Ten more minutes. Perfection takes time, ladies." Jared wiped barbeque sauce on his chef's apron. "Bring out the salads, and don't forget the wine Doug brought. It's sitting on the counter."

The picnic table was cluttered with overflowing trays and bowls of food as Jared placed a steak on each plate.

"Before you animals dig in, I would just like to say I'm thrilled to be back. I love and missed you all very much," Jamie said and lifted her glass of wine.

"Here, here," everyone said in unison, clanking glasses together.

"Now pass the potatoes," Sam said.

Jamie couldn't help but smile as she glanced around the table, observing everyone laughing and enjoying themselves.

Relaxed and easy as though they did this every weekend. She knew now she needed more days like this one. Just hanging out in a yard was a luxury. She thought of her parents, particularly her dad who used to barbeque in the evenings. She was overcome with a longing for her family she hadn't felt in a long time.

"We need napkins," she heard Alex say.

"I'll get them," Doug said.

She watched Doug as he rose to his feet. For a moment, she studied Doug intently, trying not to get caught staring at him.

"Hello, can you pass the potatoes, please?" Sam asked.

"Yeah, sorry," Jamie said.

"You okay? You've been drifting off a lot." Sam asked.

"Yeah, just nostalgia, I guess," Jamie said, forcing her thoughts back to the present.

*   *   *

Sam started clearing the picnic table. "I knew you boys had some talent," she joked, tossing Remy a piece of meat, not wanting to disappoint him as he lay under the picnic table hoping for a few spills. "I'll take the dishes in, and then I'm hitting the shower."

"After that meal, I could use a walk. Anyone interested?" Doug asked.

"I'm up for it," Jamie volunteered.

Jared shook his head. "You go ahead, I've got to feed the animals, then I'm heading in to catch the end of the Indians."

"I'll join you for that game," Sam said.

"What about you?" Jamie asked Alex.

"You guys go ahead; I have to get up early tomorrow to catch up on chores. Go enjoy your walk," Alex said.

*   *   *

After walking along the dirt road and back, Doug asked, "Where to next?"

"Let's go over by the pond and sit by the water."

They had been talking as if they had never been apart. Everything felt so easy between them. But Jamie sensed something serious in Doug. She knew he would ask about why she had left. I'm just not ready, she thought.

Doug and Jamie walked in silence until they found a rock to sit on near the water's edge. Anywhere near the woods made Jamie uneasy but the pond felt okay.

"Are you feeling all right? You're kind of pale."

"I'm fine. It's just been a long day."

"It certainly has."

They both stared out the water, the evening wind rippling the pond water. The quiet was almost comfortable between them.

And easily as if they had never left, Doug took Jamie's hand in his.

"I missed you, Jamie."

Jamie felt as if the whole world could hear her heart beating. She looked up into his eyes but saw more than just lust. She saw the pain she had caused him all those years before.

"I'm sorry but I have to ask," Doug said. "Why did you just pick up and leave? No note, no call, no nothing. I kind of thought we'd be spending our lives together." He looked at her in the waiting silence.

"It was a long time ago, Doug. We're different people now. I can tell you my leaving had nothing to do with you. It's just something I don't really care to talk about now."

"Have dinner with me tomorrow night, and I'll leave the past in the past. Deal?" Doug spoke again when he saw her hesitation.

"Friends hanging out and catching up on old times, one meal. I would like to hear what you've been up to; I heard you're a big shot now." He needed answers but knew this wasn't the time or place. Not yet anyway. He'd waited ten years. He could wait a little longer. After all, she'd only been back a day.

"I've got to eat, so might as well as let you pick up the tab," she chuckled.

CHAPTER 6

Jamie pushed and prodded to no avail, trying to pry open the old window in what used to be Alex's childhood bedroom. The temperature seemed to rise as she tossed and turned in bed. After a couple of hours, she accepted defeat and opted for a cold shower and a glass of ice water. Getting any sleep didn't seem to be an option again tonight, or any night since she'd been here for that matter.

After cooling off, she curled up in front of a fan she found in the closet, and her thoughts wandered—first of the evening that just passed and then of her upcoming date. Finally, she drifted off to sleep.

And in her sleep, her nightmares ran free. She didn't mean to do anything wrong. She'd walked to the clubhouse that day, just as she had a million times. The quiet, the peace, it was her escape with, and sometimes without, her friends. It gave her time to think, daydream, and plan. That day seemed somehow different from the minute she got there—eerily quiet. An oddly primitive warning sounded in her brain. Considering the sunny, pleasant day, she didn't feel right, and her instincts told her something was wrong. That's probably why she decided to leave as soon as she had arrived. The sun was too bright, and she squinted, holding up her hands to protect herself, running away from the light.

"Doug, please help! Don't let him hurt me again! STOP!" Jamie awoke shouting. She lay on the floor sobbing in a ring of sweat. Icy fear twisted around her heart. She looked up to see Remy licking her face with affection.

Jamie quickly scanned the room, thankful no one had heard her. "Just a bad nightmare."

*   *   *

The smell of the fresh brewed coffee found its way up the stairs and stirred Jamie's senses. She finished buttoning her blouse, swiped a brush through her hair, and was preparing to head downstairs for a cup when she heard a bird chirping so loudly, it sounded like it was in the room with her. She glanced over to see that the window she couldn't open was now cracked about three inches. A chill passed through her.

She quickly quelled her fear. Jared had probably walked in and opened the window for her.

"Move it, people," Jared said. "We don't sleep until noon around here. Up with the roosters, let's go."

"He gets off on this stuff," Sam griped, half asleep and stumbling down the stairs.

"Move it, Conner, the animals will starve waiting for you," Jared said to Sam.

Jamie was assigned to assist Jared all day with the hay, and she knew he'd work her like a dog until every muscle in her body ached with pain, and she couldn't wait.

*   *   *

Jamie was about ready to just go naked if these two girls made her change into one more outfit. She was only going to eat at a small restaurant on the beach with Doug, a friend. After all, she had only said yes to get him to stop asking so many questions.

"What do you think, Alex?" Samantha asked.

"It works," Alex nodded. "Jamie, you look beautiful."

"It's about time. You'd think I was going to the prom the way you two are acting." Jamie tried to brush her hair out of her face to no avail.

Samantha grabbed the brush from her hand and in a flash had her hair piled on the side of her head with a matching butterfly pin to secure it in place.

At last, she was downstairs and on the porch while she waited for Doug. All her toes and fingers were blistered from the day's work, but she felt great. The added bonus was her new sun-drenched complexion.

Jamie rested on the porch swing as Doug drove up the drive. Remy was the first to greet him, barking and wagging his tail in excitement. Jared walked out from the barn to see what all the racket was about and started whistling.

"Jeez, what's going on here, you don't ever get Betsy out for me. Is there something I need to know?" he smiled, throwing a friendly punch.

At this point everyone had gathered on the porch to see them off, and Jamie wasn't thrilled with all the attention. Jamie had noticed Doug was even starting to blush.

"So what's everyone up to tonight?" Jamie asked.

"Oh, we're gonna sit around and get drunk, and wait for you two to come home so we can interrogate you," Samantha said.

"By the way, I'm having dinner tomorrow. I'd like everyone to be here at 6 p.m. sharp," Alex said. "I have someone I'd like everyone to meet. Doug, that includes you, too."

"Yes, ma'am. I'll be there, me and my appetite," Doug said.

Jared looked at his sister. "Is this a boyfriend we're meeting? When did this happen?"

"You'll just have to come and see." Alex smiled and walked back in the house.

"Well, it looks like this is the week of surprises. Shall we go?" Jamie asked. As an afterthought, she put her arm around Doug's just to get a rise out of everyone.

*   *   *

Jamie was surprised at how much fun she was having. She loved the continuous rows of corn fields, the enormous amount of trees, all that green. Several men were fishing along the creek. She had even spotted a few deer feeding by the outer edges of the woods. None of it was part of her daily routine anymore, and she hadn't realized she'd missed it until now.

At the restaurant, they had talked for two hours at the patio table before getting around to ordering. Doug talked about Haley and how proud he was of her and the perils of being a single dad. She could tell how he tried to make up for the fact that Haley didn't have a mother figure. He told her what life had been like with Amy, about the day she left, and how he thanked God everyday that she didn't take Haley with her. They talked about his parents and how Haley had brought them all closer together.

After finishing their desserts, they decided to go for a walk along the beach.

"It's been nice seeing you, Jamie," he said as he let his hand slip into hers, and they walked barefooted through the water, grains of sand sticking to their feet. "You look great tonight, by the way. With all the commotion back at the house I didn't get to tell you."

"Thanks, you don't look so bad yourself," she said, managing a small, tentative smile.   She swatted a mosquito on her leg. She'd forgotten how pesky those things were.

"You okay?" Doug asked.

"I'm fine. Bug bite." Jamie pointed to the red spot on her leg. "So, do you know anything about this mystery guest we're meeting tomorrow?"

"I don't, and from Jared's expression, he doesn't either. I haven't seen her with anybody. She's gone a lot, but she's usually working on a project with the animals or at the fairgrounds, stuff like that."

"I guess we'll find out tomorrow. She's had this wicked twinkle in her eye lately. Also, she has been more outspoken than usual. He must be special if—"

Jamie felt the cold water drip down her legs. "Hey!"

Doug laughed at her shock. He splashed water at her again.

Then they were both laughing and splashing each other. Jamie drank

in the comfort of his nearness. With a giddy sense of pleasure, she

let her happiness show.

*   *   *

That son of a bitch. What the hell does he think he's doing

with her? She was his. Coming over to the farm was one thing.

Getting out of his sports car, flaunting his money around, and

pushing her to go to dinner with him is entirely a different matter

and not to be tolerated. Look at him. Touching her. Holding her

hand. Flirting with her on the beach. It was sickening.

Jamie's job was to start adding to the family. He could

picture it, both of them with a handful of children running around the

cabin that he had built for her. Jamie folding laundry and serving

dinner as he relaxed with a glass of fresh lemonade on the porch. It

got him excited just thinking about it.

But with this other guy, his plan was going to have to be

altered. He had a lot of thinking to do.

*   *   *

"I'd like ten minutes alone with the bastard who did this. No respect for a man's property. Any decent person knows this isn't how you settle scores," Jared said. His eyes blazed amber fire as he stood around Doug's car, still amazed at what he saw in front of him.

"He sure did some damage. Angry about something," Doug said. His expression darkened with fury.

When Jamie and Doug came back to the car from dinner, both were shocked to see 'Asshole stay away from her or else' scratched onto his hood, all four tires sliced. Jared came into town to give them a lift and help Doug with the task of getting the vehicle back to the farm.

Back at the farm, the girls gathered around the kitchen table, listening intently to Jamie.

"It was a perfect evening until we came out to the car." Jamie shifted the salt shaker back and forth in her hand. She was frightened. Was this her attacker out of hiding?

Someone had been watching them.

"It could be anything from mistaken identity to random vandalism." Sam placed her hand on Jamie's shoulder.

Jamie thought about telling the girls her terrible history but she didn't want to say anything until she knew for sure. No reason to stir things up now.

"There's nothing you can do about it. Stop worrying, Jamie. It was probably some drunk teenagers out for a little fun," Alex said. She leaned across the table. "Let's talk about good things. What's the next step with you and Doug?"

"There isn't any next step." Jamie stood up. She was hardly ready to talk about her feelings for Doug. She didn't really know herself. "I need a minute," Jamie said and walked out to the porch to be alone.

She couldn't remember the last time she'd truly enjoyed the company of a man. But she couldn't pull Doug into her life. Not when she would have to ask him to choose between her and more family. The rapist had left her damaged in more ways than one. It would be too complicated. And she wasn't the girl she used to be.

She heard voices and noticed the sheriff had arrived to make an official report.

"Do you have any idea who did this?" the sheriff asked.

Both men shook their heads.

Bobby Mason Jr. was the local sheriff in town. He took over for his dad when he retired. Bobby went to school with them, and Doug and Bobby played together on the football team. He had worked on the force since he'd graduated. Married his high school sweetheart, Jackie, and had three girls. He brought them out to the farm occasionally to ride the horses and play with the animals.

"Try to remember anybody out of the ordinary you saw or talked to. Any small detail could help. In the meantime, I would keep an eye on the girls. I'll get this report filed after I talk to the employees at the restaurant and see if there's any witnesses. I'll drop off a copy of the report to you in a few days so you can file it with your insurance. If you think of anything else, give me a call."

"Sure thing. Thanks, Bobby. Are we gonna see you and the family at the clambake in a few weeks?" Jared asked.

"Wouldn't miss it. The girls are already talking about it," he said.

*   *   *

Shit! He had been too enraged to think straight. He needed to be more careful. Someone could have seen him scratching on that bastard's car.

But on the other hand, his beloved now knew he was around.

He wanted to shout out, "Jamie, I'm here for you now." He knew he

could make her love him. He would.

CHAPTER 7

Alex finished setting the table. She had incorporated

everyone's favorites into a huge feast. Slowly cooked pot roast with

carrots, potatoes, mushrooms, and onions, garlic toast, Caesar salad,

broccoli and cheese rice, and a homemade cherry and apple pie for

dessert with ice cream. Fresh-picked flowers from the garden

provided a colorful centerpiece. She had set out her mom's china,

her great grandmother's lace tablecloth, and she went to the cellar

and picked up a couple bottles of wine.

Everyone was on the sun porch having a before-dinner drink

when a blue Chevy pickup 4x4 pulled up the gravel drive. A woman

jumped out. She had on a pair of Wrangler jeans and a Thorton's

Farm t-shirt, a white cowboy hat, and a pair of cowboy boots. Alex sauntered out of the house in a pink cotton skirt and a white blouse.

"Awful spiffy," Jared said to Doug low enough so that Alex wouldn't hear, "just to have a friend over."

"Everyone, this is Cristal Johansen. A friend of mine I met last year during the cattle auction at the county fair. Cristal was one of the judges and also volunteered at the stands," Alex said.

"Like a beer?" Sam asked.

"Wine, if you have it," Cristal said.

"Merlot," Alex said and smile. "I have some in the kitchen for everyone. Oh, and dinner is ready."

Alex led the way. Sam, Jamie, and Cristal sat on one side, Jared, Doug, and herself on the other. She had chosen the formal dining room—a rare event indeed.

"Wow, this looks pretty tasty," Jared said as he lifted the lid to the roast and took a whiff. The aroma filled the air.

Everyone bowed their heads while Doug had the honors of saying grace. Seconds later, dishes and bowls were being passed in all directions. Halfway through the meal, Alex poured everyone a glass of wine and stood up.

"If I could have everyone's attention, please. I have an announcement to make," Alex said.

"Everyone has met Cristal," she said as she walked over and stood next to her. "I've called all of you together today because I've made some tough decisions, and all of you here are an important part of my life. I would like to include you on some choices I've made and ask for your support. Cristal and I have been dating for close to a year now. I've asked her to move in with me."

"All of you are very important to Alex," Cristal said and stood up beside Alex. "We feel it's important to share this gift we've been given and ask you for your blessing." Cristal clasped Alex's hand in hers.

Alex scanned the table, visibly shaking.

Jared had stiffened up, and he stared emptily at Cristal.

Sam had apparently decided they needed more than wine and brought a six-pack of beer from the fridge. In her other hand was a bottle of Jack.

Sam then handed a beer to the guys, which they gratefully accepted along with a swig of Jack.

Doug grabbed the platter of pot roast to start on seconds. He threw another piece of bread on his plate, ignoring the looks he was getting from Jared. He focused on his food.

Alex sat back down and nodded for Cristal to do the same. She was hoping they could just start eating and move on. She grabbed a platter of potatoes from the table and dished a pile onto her plate, then handed it over to Cristal.

"Cristal, is your family from around here?" Jamie asked.

"Actually, about a couple hours from here over in—"

"I am not going to sit here and fucking pretend like this is a dinner at the Walton's!" Jared stood up and threw down napkin. He gave Alex a sidelong glance of utter disbelief as he continued. "Alex, I thought more of you than this. And you've been running around, lying and sneaking for a year! Not to mention the twisted, disgusting idea of it all. I'm not gonna take part in any of it." He grabbed the rest of the six-pack, the bottle of Jack, and charged out the door.

"I'll go talk to him," Doug volunteered. "You just took us all by surprise. You know your brother, he's never been big on change." On his way out, he turned to Cristal. "Nice to meet you. I hope Alex gave you some warning on what you're in for." And he headed out to the barn to find Jared.

*   *   *

Jamie and Samantha cleared the table while Cristal went to console Alex who had gone to room after Jared left. Jamie wasn't sure what to think. Especially coming from Alex. She was the stable one, holding down her parents' farm, staying in her hometown. There was never any gossip to spread about her. A few dates here and there with some local farmers. She dated one of the Meade boys, Matt, for a couple of years, but she broke it off and never really spoke of it much.

Jamie and Sam were the ones throwing curve balls. Running off, getting married, getting divorced, doing their own thing. Alex had never thrown Jared a curve ball.

"I don't get what the big deal is," Samantha said, breaking the silence. "It is the new millennium after all. Besides, it was about time Alex did some shaking up around here."

"True enough," Jamie said.

"Cristal seems respectable enough." Cristal owned a ranch about an hour from Alex's house. Graduated from Ohio State

University and had earned an agriculture degree. Judged at the local

fairs, trained children how to show animals, and sponsored the 4-H

Chapter. She also served as a co-chairman for the County Fair. And

once a week mentally challenged children came out to her ranch to

ride, feed, and help learn to care for the horses. "Male, female,

whatever. As long as Cristal treats Alex well and doesn't break her

heart, she's got my vote."

The girls, satisfied with the clean up, pulled Cristal and Alex

downstairs and headed out to the porch to play quarters, a drinking

game from their high school days. Jamie put an old AC/DC tape in

the radio and "Back in Black" blared from the speakers. Sam

grabbed the tequila, beer, and shot glasses.

*   *   *

After throwing darts in the barn, Doug had calmed Jared

down, and Jared was somewhat listening to reason. He was still

pissed at Alex for hiding this from him, but Doug had a few valid

points. She was an adult. Able to make her own decisions. She

always had covered for him and supported him.

Her turn to ask for support was well past due. He at least

owed her that much. He would talk to Cristal and see what kind of person she was, but the whole moving-in thing needed to wait awhile. He had always envisioned Alex getting married and having children. Obviously she had other plans.

Jared was ready to try it again. Remy practically mowed him and Doug down as he accompanied them, eager to lead the way to the porch. Remy was a big old baby and hid under the barn, far from any confrontations. He must have felt safe now because he was wagging his tail as he leaped up on to Alex's lap, giving her a big, sloppy kiss. Jared, not far behind, heard the blaring music and took a look at the shot glasses and quarters on the table and knew it would be a long night.

*   *   *

Doug had downed his third shot, and just shared with everyone that he wore boxer brief combos, and realized he would feel about eighty in the morning. He'd already agreed to sleep on the couch tonight. There was no way he was driving, and since Haley was with his parents, he could stay out and play a little bit. Which was something rare these days.

Next was Jamie's turn. Every time her gaze met his, his heart turned over in response. She lined up her quarter, bounced it off the table, and barely missed the shot glass by a half an inch.

"Drink, drink, drink!" everyone shouted and pounded the table in unison as she guzzled the beer.

*　　　*　　　*

The early morning sun flooded the living room with bright light, making it impossible for Doug to sleep in. He made a feeble attempt to lift a pillow over his head to no avail. He lay there for about a half hour and finally surrendered. The longer he lay there, the more his thoughts drifted to Jamie. He slipped into his pants and went to the kitchen to brew a pot of coffee. They would all be needing it. He reached for his head and held it tight as if that would stop the throbbing. Tylenol. There had to be some around here, he thought as he opened and closed peach-colored cabinets until he found what he was looking for.

Doug decided to make some eggs, bacon, potatoes, and grabbed a bag of bread for toast. He was just about finished when Jared stumbled down the stairs with Cristal right behind him. He handed each of them a cup of coffee and started filling a plate for each of them. He figured the smell of coffee and grease would draw the others down soon.

As the three of them were finishing their meal, the girls came down the stairs. Sam snatched the coffee. Alex grabbed the plates and handed them out. Jamie threw a couple more pieces of toast in the toaster. Not much was said. Everyone shared their misery in silence.

Cristal dragged herself to the sink to wash her hands. They still reeked of tequila, lemon, and salt. She glanced out the window and down again to her hands. It took a minute to register. She took a second look to be sure. "Um, guys, there's a fleet of pigs in the backyard being chased around by Remy."

"My, my, still the humorous one this morning. I thought the comedy routine last night was the alcohol talking," Jared said, going along with her joke as he munched on a piece of toast.

"No, I'm being serious. I wasn't sure either, but I kid you not. There's Remy chasing a dozen or so really big pigs." Cristal pointed to the south end of the property.

"We don't have any pigs," Alex chimed in.

"I know that, silly. That's why I'm pointing it out."

Doug bent over from the stove and took a look. "Yep, those are pigs," he said and went back to cooking.

"So now we're all being funny," Jared said. But even as he did, he went to look out the window. "Shit, there are pigs in the backyard, a mess of 'em, too."

"Looks like breakfast is over." Doug turned off the burner and put on his boots.

"Alex, call over to the Mitchell's and tell them their damn pigs are over here. We'll try and round them up. Keep Remy from causing too much havoc," Jared said and headed out the door behind Doug.

"Isn't the Mitchell place a good two or three miles down the road?" Jamie asked.

"Yeah, maybe a little farther. Happened one other time about five years ago, only two got out then. Has to be theirs, no one else around here raises pigs," Alex said, dialing the phone.

"That's something else, all of them down here together," Jamie said.

"I'm gonna go help. It'll get my mind off this hangover," Cristal said.

"I'm going too," Jamie said, then added, "but not to help. I just want to watch."

"Yeah, me too," Sam said, running out barefooted.

"Great, don't mind me. I'll work on this." Alex looked around at the cluttered table and bacon sizzling on the stove.

After breakfast and wrestling pigs into a truck, the guys spent the day shopping for parts for piecing Betsy back together while the girls cleaned up the mess of last night's escapades. When they finished, Cristal left to run some errands, and the girls retreated to the back patio for some sun and most importantly, a much-needed nap.

"Want to go for a jog later? All this food and alcohol isn't going to help my figure or my health any," Jamie asked the girls.

"Not me. I don't jog, sorry," Sam said.

"After our nap, Cristal and I are driving out to her house and packing some of her things. Jared and I had a long talk last night. I agreed to give him time to adjust and get acquainted with Cristal before any further steps. Jared agreed to let Cristal live at the farm part of the week, so he doesn't lose his baby sister yet." Said Alex.

"I guess I'm on my own then," Jamie said.

*   *   *

She was running back and forth on the dirt road leading to the farm. He wanted her to come closer. Come to the woods, my dear, he wanted to call. He knew she would eventually. She couldn't stay away forever.

CHAPTER 8

Everyone was about ready for the annual Hometown Summer

Festival. The city was blocked off. In place of cars were food and

beer stands, flea market booths, games, rides, softball tournaments,

and many other events. The air was filled with scents of roasted

peanuts and fried foods. The once quiet streets meshed with crowds

of people and vendor booths. The sounds of Travis Trent blared from the speakers. Jamie sat on the bleachers, a softball mitt

perched on her lap.

Doug had persuaded everyone into playing on his softball

team he sponsored every year as advertisement for his business. She

still wasn't too keen on the idea. She hadn't played softball in over

ten years. She had visions of getting clobbered upside the head with

a line drive. She was outnumbered though. Everyone else,

including Cristal, thought it was an excellent idea. Maybe she'd get

lucky and no ball would come her way, but then there was the

batting situation. She actually snuck into town earlier in the week

and practiced at the batting cage for a couple of hours. After fifty

attempts, she got lucky and hit one. She made contact with a few

more after that, but certainly nothing to brag about. She just wanted

to keep from being embarrassed or being the main reason for a loss.

It would be entertaining and a much-deserved break. Ever

since last weekend's drunk fest, Jared had been working everyone to

the bone. Doug handled repairs around the house. The rest of the

group were assigned chores on the farm: feeding, cleaning the

animals, mowing the grass, pulling weeds, tending to the garden,

watering flowers, bailing hay, whatever he could find.

The excruciating pain in Jamie's lower back was proof enough of the dawn-to-dusk schedule she'd kept all week. New calluses and torn skin marked her hands. She certainly didn't have to worry about missing her exercise regimen now. Fatigue lingered within her, but she also felt fit and fulfilled.

They did manage to find time for a swim here and there in the pond out back. And the girls often stayed up late. Somehow the conversations always strayed back to Doug. Despite Jamie's best efforts to avoid the subject, something kept drawing her in. It had to do with his wholesome everyday peace. Jamie had promised herself to not think about Doug. That proved more difficult than she had imagined, especially with the girls around.

"Why in the hell would you order pink shirts for a softball game? You expect us to win the series in pink freakin' shirts? This isn't the powder puff girls. Jesus, Doug, these are hideous!" Jared said.

"Just put the damn thing on and shut up. Besides, it's not pink, it's apricot, but I prefer off-orange. That's all they had left at the last minute when the others dropped out."

"You're banned from uniform assignment from this point forward. I don't care if we have to order camouflage or order them from New York. No more pink," Jared said.

"You're driving me nuts. We're here to play ball not win a fashion show," Sam said.

"Listen up, everyone," Doug called out. "I have here your positions and batting order." He handed a copy to everyone.

The first team was a group from the local bank, and both Doug and Jared thought they had a decent chance to win.

*   *   *

"Nice hustle, Jamie. Way to catch those balls out there," one of the guys from the other team yelled as she stood in line for a sandwich.

She peaked out from under her baseball cap and nodded a thanks. She smiled to herself. She was covered in dust and had banged up her left knee sliding into third. They had won two games in row and now had a bye. They were done for the night and were still in the winner's bracket. It was time for fun and food.

She grabbed a chilidog and homemade French fries. She was off to the dunking booth where Doug had been conned into donating his time. He served as a member of the volunteer fire department. Every year they sponsored the dunking booth to raise money for community projects and children events.

She couldn't wait. She wanted to make sure she was the first one to get a toss.

Jared and Sam went back over to the softball field to spy on the competition. They both were taking this tournament very serious. The competition would steadily rise over the next two days. Jamie noticed they walked away hand in hand. They were getting pretty close for just being friends, she thought.

Cristal and Alex volunteered to help with a kid's petting zoo. It was the first year they were trying it. Both Alex and Cristal lent some animals and were going to help out for a couple of hours.

Jamie was on her own, cheering on the players as they attempted to knock Doug off of his seat. She threw the first five balls with no success. So, she cheated and grabbed another ball and stood about five feet from the bull's-eye. Down he went. Jamie wanted to make sure she was the first one to soak him. She gave him a wink and threw an extra twenty into the collection box.

As Doug climbed back up on his perch, she called to him. "I'm going to see if I can find any familiar faces. Can I meet you back here in a couple of hours?" Jamie asked.

"Sure, we'll go on some rides. Maybe I'll even win you a big stuffed bear." He smiled. "Just give me enough time to change. I'll meet you over by the lockers," Doug said.

Jamie browsed around the booths, remembering how much fun she used to have at festivals. She went to the Taste of Chicago a few times, but nothing compared to the comfort of a small hometown get-together. She scribbled her name on several coupons for drawings. She bought a beer mug, a couple cheap bracelets, a t-shirt, a pair of sunglasses, cotton candy, and some toys for Haley including a yo-yo, a kid's purse, some string foam, and jewelry to put in the purse.

She hadn't even met Haley yet and found the need to make a great impression. Haley would be home in time for the clambake next week. She knew it was important to Doug that she meet her. The truth was she was looking forward to it. Haley was important to

Doug. He talked about her often, but where did she fit in all of this? After all, she would be back to Chicago in a couple weeks. It was ironic when she thought about it. She hadn't missed work, hadn't even called to check in on their progress. For years that's all she had done was put everything into her work. It was what defined her. Kept her going. It was who she was. She had to remember it was a vacation. Just a vacation.

Children jostled into her, and she came out of her reverie. Kids were everywhere—being towed in wagons or dragged along to the next booth. Parents tried to soothe the constant yells of joy and exhaustion. It sounded of comfort and family to her.

Looking at her watch, she realized she still had a lot of time on her hands and wandered into one of the local bars on the strip, "The Cold One," and ordered a Bud Lite and a glass of ice. The bar was decorated in Cleveland Indians paraphernalia. They had four pool tables in one room, a stage, and the main bar area. The place was packed and smelled of grease, smoke, and stale beer. The floor was covered with cracked peanut shells. The cool air was a needed break from the hot, humid outdoors.

She recognized some of the patrons and chitchatted for a few minutes before continuing on. Digging in her pocket for quarters, she placed three on the pool table. She played often when she was younger. Jamie racked the balls when it was her turn. Her opponent was John, a guy from school. He had been a couple of grades behind her. She walked over to the outdated jukebox. She briefly studied the song list, then inserted a five-dollar bill, and selected several upbeat songs. She always played better when she went along with the rhythm.

"You want to play for a drink?" John asked Jamie.

"Sure," she said as she selected the heaviest pool stick she could find from the rack and chalked the tip.

John broke the balls and hit in a stripe. Then missed his next shot. She was used to guys underestimating her ability before they saw her play. She still played occasionally at work functions, since her boss had a pool table in his basement.

She reviewed her options and then hit in a couple of easy shots. The three ball bounced off two ends of the table and into the pocket, then she missed her next one. The straight-in ones seemed to be tougher than the challenging shots for her. After that she ran the table. It was all coming back. She could envision the ball going in,

and where to hit it.

"Nice," John said, sounding surprised. She wound up

beating him two games in a row and was playing the next challenger

at this point, who upped the ante to five dollars a game, which she

accepted. She easily beat him with just two turns.

When she was getting ready to break for her next game, she

had an odd feeling someone was watching her. Not again. What

was with her these days?

Her nerves tensed immediately. Her heart was beating

rapidly, and she had trouble catching her breath. Her hairs were

standing straight up. What was wrong with her? She was on the

verge of a panic attack.

She caught herself glancing uneasily over her shoulder. As

she did so, a warning voice went off in her head. She tried to calm

herself down and just play the game. She looked out of the corner of

her eye and quickly scanned the room. Her eyes locked for a brief

moment with someone else staring right back at her from the other

end of the bar. It was only a split second of eye contact, but it felt

like five minutes.

Jamie couldn't make out who it was, but he was definitely watching her, and she didn't like it. Her stomach was jittery. She tried to get another subtle glance at him. She was sure it was nothing.

But when she looked over again, there was no doubting the fact he was watching her, staring at her. She couldn't make out a full description, but he had a mousy look to him. His hair was jet black. So much to the point it almost had a purple tint to it and was matted to his head. She also saw he had glasses on, and was a little shorter than her. He had on a long-sleeved shirt and a heavy pair of polyester pants, which was odd considering it was well over ninety degrees out.

"Are you gonna shoot or what?" her competitor asked.

She swallowed hard, trying to manage a feeble answer.

"Yeah, sorry." She grabbed a swig of beer and tried to focus on the music and her pool shot. Jamie took in several deep breaths to calm her nerves, but she could still feel his eyes on her. The nagging in the back of her mind refused to be stilled. She hit a couple balls in and missed the next one. So, someone was looking a little too long, big deal.

Maybe it was someone from school or the community who thought they recognized her, but didn't want to come over and say "hi" unless they were sure. That was probably it. Something simple. Yet, her instincts told her different. She kept glancing in his direction. Not only was he glaring at her, he was slowly moving closer with a disturbing grin on his face. She strained to get a good look. It was hard to focus with the blinking beer signs that were hung up on the walls behind him. His whole look was repulsive to her.

She couldn't make out details or see his eyes; everything seemed fuzzy. He was too far away, and she was worried about looking too long. She didn't want to invite him to approach her.

She felt danger and threw down her stick and decided she was leaving now. She apologized to the gentleman who was her opponent, handed him a five-dollar bill, and mumbled something about being late. The bar was completely packed. She had to shove her way through the crowd, doing her best not to panic. Halfway from the door, Jamie was at a dead stop trying to edge her way out of the jam when she felt someone clench the back of her shirt. The touch terrified her. Causing a cold-like sweat to drip down her forehead. Her face instantly turned a pale ashen-like color. That direct contact had a familiar feel to it. A dreadful one. She choked back the old fears.

What happened next seemed like a blur. Someone tugged on her hair. With certainty, she knew it was the guy staring at her. She yelled, "No!" and began flailing her arms around hysterically and bolted, thrusting for the door. Horrific images were flashing thought her head. Visions. The knot in the pit of her stomach tightened. She had to get outside. Had to breathe. The guy in front of her stepped aside, shielding her from the crowd, allowing an opening for her to get to the door.

"Are you okay," the guy asked.

She just shook her head and bolted out the door. He blocked everyone from following her. Before he could speak, she was gone, running down the main drag.

*   *   *

Jamie met Doug by the lockers. She did everything she could to look calm. She didn't want to alarm him or involve him in any way. She still didn't understand what had happened really. Did she imagine it all up? She took a long deep breath and counted to ten, then let it out. She splashed some water on her face from the fountain to help combat the heat and faintness she was feeling.

Doug stopped dead in his tracks when he saw her face. Jamie looked like she was going to fall on the floor any minute. She was trembling, and her eyes had a horrifying, hypnotic look in them.

"Are you sick? What's wrong?" He slid his arm around her, fearing she would pass out.

"I'm okay."

Doug interrupted, "Tell me what the hell happened. You're a mess. Please, let me in so I can help you."

"Something did happen. We will talk, I promise. But tonight, I just need to be with you," she pleaded. "There's no way I can take anymore right now."

He thought about it for a minute. He was concerned, but this was as close as he'd gotten to any answers. So he would wait until tomorrow.

"Okay. You have a deal, tomorrow. No backing out. Agreed?" Doug asked.

Jamie nodded in agreement.

"Are you sure you're all right? We can always go home if you're not feeling up to it," he asked.

"No, I've been looking forward to this all week. Let's go for that ride on the Ferris wheel," she said, grabbing Doug's hand.

*   *   *

"It's breathtaking from here, looking down on everything. The people, the trees, the lake, all so peaceful from the sky, so small," Jamie said. She relaxed with her head leaning against Doug's chest. She had longed for the protectiveness of his arms. Waiting at the top for the ride to begin as others were still being seated, they rocked peacefully back and forth to the sounds of the creaking of the wheel. They had already ridden several rides and had saved their favorite for last. Next to her, she had an oversized stuffed dolphin Doug had won throwing baseballs at a bull's-eye.

It had turned out to be a favorable evening considering everything. She didn't allow herself to think about anything but the moment at hand. She was comfortable and secure where she was. Here with Doug. They watched the boats out on the lake.

"Thank you," she said. He made her feel good. She was glad to be with him.

"For what?" he asked.

"For your patience, your friendship, and for tonight. I needed it."

"You're welcome," he said as he studied her eyes. He gave her a small kiss on the lips. Doug couldn't have been any happier than he was at this moment. He tried not to think it would disappear again soon.

"For old times," he said. They both sat hand-in-hand quietly relishing the moment.

CHAPTER 9

On the boat he borrowed, he watched them together. Arms locked on the Ferris wheel. Doug even had the gall to kiss her, and it pissed him off. Seeing them all lovey-dovey was making him sick. That should be him cuddling with her on the rides.

He laid the binoculars down, deciding to take a cigarette break before he got too upset. He grabbed the pack out of his shirt pocket. Lighting one up, he inhaled deeply as he reminded himself to be patient. She would be his soon enough.

He considered the boat borrowed, because the people who owned it wouldn't need it any longer. He hadn't meant to kill them. The lady wouldn't quit screaming, and people were starting to notice. He just wanted the boat. He knew they were from Chicago because they had it painted on the side. It was obviously used for fishing because there was equipment scattered throughout the boat that was in his way. He thought about throwing it overboard and decided against it. He could use the fishing gear as a decoy to avoid any suspicion.

He wanted an out-of-town boat so no one would miss it right away. He had planned on just tying them up and discarding them down below. She wouldn't shut up. Kept screaming, kicking, spitting, and biting. Not listening to him. Why wouldn't women just listen? Life would be so much easier if they just did as they were told. None of them obeyed, not her, not his mother, and certainly not Jamie. You had to make them listen. Whatever happened was their fault. It could all be avoided if they knew their place and kept their mouths shut.

He needed a boat for easy access in and out of the festival and to keep an eye on his love. Maybe he could get the boat painted and keep it. It would make a nice wedding gift. It was roomy, well-equipped, and ran smooth. She would like that, wouldn't she? Great for family vacations with Jamie and their children. It would allow them privacy, which was very important to him. He didn't want people around digging into their business. That was part of the problem now. All her damn nosey friends telling her how things should be, who she should be with, and where she should live.

He looked down at the dead bodies lying in the galley. Work. That's what women created was work. Now he would have to drag the bodies out and find a place to bury them. He didn't have time for such trivial tasks.

His sweetheart, his true love. All this was for her and did she appreciate it? No, she didn't.

He was only admiring her. He hadn't meant to get so close. To stare so long. He hadn't wanted her to notice him quite yet, but he couldn't help himself. She was so precious. Her skin so delicate, her sweet smell, the cute little bounce she had when she walked. He had to touch her to remember what it was like. The excitement came rushing back when he put his hand against her skin.

He wanted to say hello. To let her know he was back in her life. He was there for her now. He never meant to alarm her.

If only Doug wasn't around and in the way. This boat actually would come in handy with the adjustments he was going to have to make due to the added complications. He would let her have her fun. He had already decided the reunion would be the night she would come home to him for good. No one was going to get in the way of that, absolutely no one.

After all, she was the one nice to him in school. She took notice, she cared, she understood, ate lunch with him, had been his lab partner when no one else would. She even came to his side to make sure he was okay when those damn football airheads had beat him up and locked him in the storage room. He knew he was different. That made him better than the rest, and Jamie saw that side of him. She took care of him. Now it was his turn to repay the favor.

His mother hadn't seen it. She had left him alone, just a little boy. He never had a dad, and he knew it was his mother's fault. She probably didn't treat him right. That lazy bitch not only deserted him and took away any chance he had to have a dad, but left him with her worthless, no good brother. What kind of life was a shack in the woods with a hermit anyway? He never talked, didn't want him around, made him do all the chores. He had to steal for food and clothes. His uncle spent all his time and money drinking and gambling.

It was all because of women, his uncle always told him and never let him forget it. Women were the cause of all evil. He could still remember vividly the whores his uncle would bring in and out of the shack. He didn't have TV, video games, family outings, or bedtime stories. No, he never had the luxuries others had, but he never used that as an excuse. Look at him now. What he wanted he took. He almost had it all, and soon he would have everything.

He could recall his uncle's words, "Boy, no one ain't gonna do nothin' for ya. You gotta do it for yourself. No one will ever give a shit about ya if you ain't a man. Women like a man with authority. Gotta let 'em know who's in charge—smack the bitch around some."

He could still see his uncle hit his whores when he was done with them. Then he would make him do stuff with them he never wanted to remember. But, he did remember all too well.

He shook his head to bring himself back to the present. That was all in the past now. He had dispensed of his uncle and that broken down shack a long time ago. There just happened to be a fire one night after his uncle passed out from one of his drunken binges. The man never could handle his whiskey. Especially not the strong stuff like tequila or Wild Turkey. He knew on those nights to stay out of the way, to try and be invisible. Only he couldn't.

He remembered his uncle shoving his finger in his face screaming and spitting. Barely able to stand up, accusing him of being as worthless as his mother. Causing him nothing but trouble and too damn expensive at that. He was old enough to start paying for himself now. Something about selling him to perverts. The yelling became louder and the poking harder. That's when it

happened. The tears poured down his cheeks.

"What the fuck you crying for, you sissy, you want

something to cry about?" his uncle said. He grabbed his head and

banged it repeatedly against the wall.

Well, he took care of that son of a bitch. He could take care

of anything else that was tossed his way. He hadn't shed a tear since

that day. Not one.

Everything he did was for her. He even built her a new cabin

and decorated it just the way she would like it. He used all her

favorite colors and fabrics. After years of research, he also knew she

favored seashells and that was the theme he used for the house. He

did it all for her, to prove his love for her.

He needed to clean up this mess, and get back to work, he

thought to himself as he inhaled one last drag of the cigarette before

tossing it to the floor and crushing it with his foot. It was essential to

his plan to spend every spare minute keeping an eye on his future

wife. He would stand in the shadows and wait. If Doug continued

to interfere, he would have no choice but to eliminate him.

CHAPTER 10

Jamie and Doug stood in line for some fudge and an elephant

ear to snack on later. They finally left and drove back to the farm.

Doug had planned to crash on Alex's couch for the weekend so he

wouldn't have to commute back and forth.

Sam and Jared filled them in on the competition they would be facing tomorrow. They had an early game in the morning, so they called it an early night.

Jamie went to bed and lay there for a while, tossing and turning. She didn't want to be alone tonight. At the same time, she didn't want to complicate things any further.

After forty-five minutes of debating, she went downstairs. She figured Doug was sleeping by now, anyway. But, when she got to the end of the staircase, she saw that he wasn't sleeping at all. She found him pacing in the living room. She stood there watching him for a few minutes. He was so handsome. She smiled at the sight of him nervously pacing back and forth. Talking to no one.

"What are you doing?" she asked. A rush of pink rose to her cheeks. She knew she had caught him in a private moment of thought.

He startled. His eyes betrayed his embarrassment at what she had seen.

Doug began to explain but she walked over and pulled him towards her, and with everything she had bottled up inside of her, pressed her lips over his and kissed him hard. She felt blood coursing through her veins like an awakened river.

At first, Doug was so shocked, his lips froze. He'd never known she was so bold. Then, instinct took over. No way was he losing this opportunity. He wrapped one arm around her and one hand slid into her hair. He consumed her with each kiss, each caress. He savored every second and wanted to keep a mental snapshot in his head of this moment forever. Each kiss tasted better than anything he could think of.

They barely came up for air. Jamie was the first to look up and gaze into his eyes. She reached for his hand and directed him towards her room. Doug paused for a moment.

"Are you sure?" Doug's voice broke with huskiness.

"I'm sure," she whispered. She led him to her room, and he followed, locking the door behind him.

"Jamie, I've missed you. There hasn't been a day that I haven't thought about you." Doug eased her onto the bed. They cuddled that way for a while, both content being in each other's arms.

First, he kissed the tip of her nose, then her eyes, and finally his lips found her mouth. "Jamie, I want to make love to you."

Jamie said nothing, but nodded as she kissed him and gasped with delight. She recklessly ripped off his shirt, the broken buttons bouncing lightly on the bed. Her mouth covered his hungrily. She allowed her tongue to explore every inch of his mouth. She pulled off his shirt and explored his chest. His touch, his kiss, the way he playfully bit her upper lip, his outdoorsy scent, everything about him felt so right.

Soon all their clothes lay haphazardly in a pile next to the bed, and Doug gently flipped her around so he was on top of her. His hand moved magically over her supple breasts, as he tasted her. His tongue made a path down her ribs to her stomach, touching and licking all the right spots as Jamie sat back with her eyes closed and enjoyed the raw passion. Doug brought Jamie to her peak and just as she was there, he stopped and started over again. It was almost more than she could bear. It had been such a long time since she had been with anyone. She hadn't experienced anything like this. Sex had always felt so good, but not like this, so alive and full of passion. The shock of him ran through her body.

He began to make love to her with everything he had inside him. Both were full of intensity, almost animal-like from anticipation.

Heat rippled under her skin. Gusts of desire shook her. He locked his fingers into hers as they moved up and down in rhythm with each other. He hungrily nibbled on her upper lip, slowing his pace down, teasing her, causing her head to spin and her body to tremble. She begged for him.

He was in no hurry. He wanted to savor every moment. He took her slowly, surely at first. Then their rhythm became hard and fast until they both came and lay in the aftermath, glowing.

Jamie snuggled against him with their legs intertwined as Doug drew her closer and held her, spooning her, and she drifted off to sleep. Doug brushed a gentle kiss across her forehead.

"I love you, Jamie, I always have."

CHAPTER 11

Jamie woke up and smiled to realize she wasn't dreaming and was lying in Doug's arms. She hadn't slept that well in a long time. She savored the feeling of satisfaction. She looked over at Doug and saw that he was awake.

"Good morning," he said and leaned over to give her a kiss.

Jamie sulked as Doug coached her out of bed and tossed her clothes to her. She was persistent in trying to convince him to stay in bed with her but he wouldn't.

"At least let me brush my teeth," she begged.

As they snuck downstairs, Jamie reached out and laced Doug's fingers with her own. They went out back and sat along the creek on a couple of big boulders. Both were silent for a few minutes, capturing the sunrise, so bright, yet serene. It was an astonishing morning.

She knew this was the time to tell Doug everything. It was burning her up, her secrets, and she was tired of keeping them from Doug.

Doug reached for a pile of stones and started skipping them across the creek, counting out loud the number of skips—a favorite pastime for both of them when they were younger. Being back in her hometown reminded her of a lot of things she used to enjoy and hadn't allowed herself to partake in over the years.

Jamie breathed in a huge sigh, held her breath, and let it out. *Okay, here it goes*, she thought. Time to put all her cards on the table.

"Doug, I know that I promised you answers, it's a lot harder than I thought."

"Just take your time. I'm here for you."

They were both quiet for a long time and then finally, she broke the silence.

"Something did happen yesterday. It wasn't really tangible, more of a feeling that opened the flood gates to a lot of bad memories. It's this strange feeling I've had since I've been here." She paused for a second, trying to arrange her thoughts to make it all come out.

"Remember when I left all those years ago, and I didn't tell you, not even a note? The next thing you hear is that I'm married, and so on and so on." Her voice had drifted off into a hushed whisper.

"Yeah, I remember."

"First, it wasn't anything to do with you. Anyway, the weekend after the festival, I went for a walk out in the woods, past the McKenzie land, over there." She pointed out into the coming sunrise. "About five miles or so back. The battered old shed that the girls and I used as a second hangout when we didn't want anyone to find us."

"Yeah, my parents told us a crazy man lived back there and to stay away," Doug said.

"We found a couple old tattered mattresses to sit on and cleaned it up a little. We kept a stereo and a few other supplies in there.

"I liked to daydream back then of how everything would turn out. I had it all down to the last detail. That's what I used to do when I wanted to be alone. I would go and daydream. Sometimes I'd climb onto the roof and soak in the sun." She shivered with the memory.

"I wasn't paying much attention. I had just gotten there. Then, out of nowhere, I got the oddest feeling I've ever had. I got a chill up and down my spine, and my hairs were standing straight up on my arms. For some reason, I was terrified. I left that place immediately. At first, I was walking fast. And then I began to run. I just needed to get out of there.

"That's when I heard noises behind me. The sound of sticks cracking as they were being smashed under footsteps. The swoosh of branches against something, someone. I was scared to look and scared not to. I tried to catch my breath enough to keep going.

"There was a man behind me about ten or twelve feet back. I couldn't make out anything about him. It was like a blur before my eyes. I knew when I saw him, I was in trouble.

"Some things I can remember with exact detail, yet some I can't recall at all. I screamed at the top of my lungs, hoping the noise would frighten him. I knew no one would hear me.

"Then, I felt his hand on my arm and he yanked me back. I fell to the ground face first. Then he climbed on top of me, his hands restraining my arms in a position that had them locked. I started kicking and screaming with all my might. Crying for help over and over. Praying someone would be around to hear me.

"'Who are you?' I cried. 'What do you want?' He said nothing. He rolled me over and as he did, I knew I had one chance before he would have me trapped again. As soon as I was facing him, I lifted my leg with all my might and swiftly went straight ahead into his groin.

"I didn't hesitate or even check to see who he was. I veered off the path because I knew it would lead me out of the woods in half the time. I was still too far of a distance away for anybody to hear me. I could hear him behind me again.

"He would cry out, 'Why are you running from me? I love you.'"

Jamie paused for a minute to catch her breath. She had been fighting tears as she told the story, but a few slipped out. She just now noticed Doug eyes were wet and red but he still held her hand clasped securely into his.

"I had taken a second too long trying to decide which way to go. He knew the woods better than I did. He pulled me down by my hair. Ripped open my top and started grabbing me, pulled down my pants and…" she looked over at Doug. "I'm not sure I should go into detail."

"I need to share this burden with you. Keep going if it helps. Please tell me anything you want."

"It does help to get it out. It's been sealed inside me too long.

"He was grabbing sticks and pushing them inside of me, preparing me for him, he had said. I remember the excruciating pain. I was raw and bloody, not sure what would happen to me. If I would even live. I struggled, not ready to accept this fate. And as he began pulling down his pants, I was able to once again get free. I knew I had to be smart. I obviously couldn't outrun him. Instead I hid on the side of a big boulder and dug in the pile of leaves a little to try and blend in.

"The sun was setting, and the last thing I wanted was to be stranded out there in the dark. I headed west, keeping me away from him, but yet closer to getting out of there. I was afraid if he caught me again, he would kill me.

"I wasn't sure how long I had been running, but I knew the clearing couldn't be much further. I was hot, covered in cold sweat, scared, filled with fear, and panic. I never saw where he was hiding. He stuck me hard in the calves, and I hit the ground and couldn't get up no matter how hard I tried. My ankles were swollen and, although I didn't know it then at the time, my leg was fractured. He made sure there was no escape. He took off his belt using one hand, sat on top of me, and with the other hand held my arms over my head. He used the belt to secure my hands. He made sure I was helpless so that he was free, to grope, poke, and slobber all over me.

"I still remember his tongue and teeth attacking my breasts like sandpaper against my skin. His lips on mine made me want to gag. He reeked of cigar smoke, sweat, and dirty laundry. I've never forgotten that stench. I felt like I'd been branded. He entered me several times from the front and back.

"My eyes were irritated and burning from the blood, and my face was caked in mud from him jamming it into the dirt with his hand. I thought I was going to die. I was barely conscious and could no longer fight. I took myself emotionally out of the present. It was the only way I could survive. It seemed like hours upon hours went by as he continued to violate me.

"Just as I felt I had nothing left in me, I felt a sharp blow to the head, and I was out cold. I awoke, not sure how long I had lain there. Then I felt the pain and remembered.

"I was so scared to move. Afraid he would there, waiting for me to awake. But he was gone. It took forever to get home. I hid behind trees and rocks whenever I heard the slightest noise. Plus my leg. When I got home, I must've stayed in the shower for three hours. I don't know how I even got home. I drove, but I don't remember doing it. I cried until I couldn't cry anymore. Then I packed my bags and left. My parents were at a cabin on the lake with friends. They never understood why I left either. I never told anyone until now.

"In one spilt second my whole life had changed. It wasn't even a choice. How could I stay and look at you, my parents, friends, or anyone in the eye? As ridiculous as it sounds, I felt I did something wrong. I had to go where no one knew me."

"Is that what had you so upset yesterday? Memories?" Doug asked.

"I think he was there, Doug. He was staring at me. He touched me. I think. I didn't look. I never did get a good visual, just the basic features. I blocked it out. I mean I saw him, but I can't picture him. I don't even know if I knew or have seen him before. It may sound strange, but when he touched me, I knew that touch. I was as petrified as I was that dreadful day in the woods.

"There have been other things too. Like the odd feeling someone's watching me. There was a closed and stuck window in my room open in the morning that I know I didn't open. I think he's out there. Then, there's your car, the graffiti, which could've been him. It's like he knows everything I do and when I do it. I'm not gonna let him scare me off this time or ruin my life. I'm just not going to let that happen."

Doug reached out to her and held her tight.

The Reunion / Page   111

"We need to see the sheriff and fill him in, Jamie. Can you do that? Not the gritty details, just a general statement. We have to catch this bastard. If there's any connection between the graffiti on my car and this psycho, then the sheriff needs to know. Not much he can probably do about a crime ten years ago. But, if there's a chance he's still after you, that could be a different story. He needs to at least be aware of the situation."

"I know, it's time to end this. Let's go in on Monday first thing."

"I'm here for you. Jamie, I wish you had told me. I would've been there for you," he said as he gently rocked her back and forth. "But, I understand." Doug paused and looked in to her eyes. "Listen, I need you to know that I love you. I always have, and I always will. I'm not going anywhere."

"I don't know what to say."

"Don't say anything right now. Just let me be here for you now."

She smiled and gave him a kiss.

"Come on, let's get some breakfast before the game. Jared's probably beside himself right now trying to find us." They both chuckled at the thought and strolled back to the house.

CHAPTER 12

Everyone was grouped around the table when Doug and Jamie ventured in the door holding hands. Everyone except Jared, that is.

"Where the hell have you two been? If we're not on the field in fifteen minutes, we'll forfeit the game and spoil our chances at the championship."

"Then let's get going." Doug grabbed a couple of pieces of toast off a plate in the kitchen, scooped some eggs and bacon on it, and handed one to Jamie. "We'll eat on the way and change when we get there," Doug said to Jamie.

Instead, everyone sat there and stared at both of them.

"What's with the handholding?" Sam asked.

"I think it's cute," Alex said.

"Enough. Save it for later. Move, let's go." Jared held the

door open and directed them out.

*   *   *

"Another round on me," Jared ordered.

Doug raised his beer. "A toast to all of us. And a special

thanks to Cristal who won the game."

"Here, here!" The team raised their glasses and toasted the

victory. They were undefeated. They had gone to the finals and

barely won in the last inning to take the series, winning the first

place trophy and $500, which was donated to the children's

community fund for parks and after school programs. Cristal had

saved the day with an almost impossible catch in right field and then

threw it all the way to the catcher to keep a tie-breaking run from

coming in and stopping a potential grand slam.

"It wasn't a big deal," Cristal said, "but thanks, I appreciate

it."

"By the way, I already have everyone penciled in for next year. The shirts already ordered," Doug said.

"It wouldn't surprise me if you did," Sam said.

Everybody laughed. She and Jared exchanged knowing glances over Doug's enthusiasm.

"Let's order. I'm starving," Doug said.

"How about some wings? We have a couple of hours before the parade begins," Jared said. Everyone nodded in agreement. Jamie looked at Doug and smiled. It felt like they had always been together.

While the others looked at the menu, she stole glances at Jared. Doug had filled Jared in on the situation, and she was going to tell the girls tomorrow. It was a question of safety for all of them now. Jamie was relieved that Jared acted as if nothing had happened, besides keeping a closer eye on her. And his one comment to her, "I'll kill the son of a bitch."

She wondered how the girls would react.

Doug had told her that they would make sure she was always with someone and never alone.

*   *   *

"Are you shitting me? That's why you left?" Sam said, her features contorted with shock and anger.

"I'm so sorry. I wish we could have been there for you." Alex wiped her eyes and handed a tissue to Jamie.

"Did anyone know?" Sam asked.

"Not until Doug yesterday."

"Why didn't you go to the police? Why didn't you tell anyone?" Sam got up and started pacing. "That guy needs to be taken down."

"And go through the horror of everyone knowing about it? I couldn't live with that invisible tag on my forehead–that poor little raped Donald girl." Her voice was shakier than she would've liked. "But now, I don't have any choice. You could be in danger."

She and Doug had driven to town earlier that morning and met with the sheriff. Without a more detailed description, there wasn't much he could do except keep an eye out for anything out of the ordinary. In a small town, any strangers would be noticed.

The sheriff also said he'd call the surrounding towns to check the computer for similar cases and possible suspects. Other than that, there wasn't much else to do.

They had a lot of work ahead of them. The regular chores around the farm had to be done, plus the clambake preparations for Saturday. All the farmers pitched in to roast a couple of pigs and buy a few kegs of beer every year. It was tradition to hold it at Jared and Alex's place. The farm had lots of room—the creek for swimming, a volleyball net, horseshoes—and it was centrally located. This year, the event fell on Jamie's birthday, so they had double reason to celebrate.

Jamie and Cristal were going shopping for supplies while Sam and Alex arranged tables, hung decorations, and organized activities. The guys were manning the pit grill and smoker, mowing the grass, and cleaning out the garage.

Jamie had a pizza date with Doug and Haley tonight, and all her nervousness slipped back to grip her. She had to laugh at the fact she was scared that a four-year-old might not like her. Doug's parents had gotten back from the lake last night to be here for the party. She knew this was important to Doug, and it was to her as well.

CHAPTER 13

Jamie rushed into the Pizza Palace a little after 7 p.m., bearing several gifts. She figured a little bribery couldn't hurt. The restaurant's limited space didn't help the sudden rush of heat that wrapped around her as she entered the building. There were rocks sitting in front of the doors to keep them perched open.

Only three of the seven or eight tables were occupied. A few people stood in the carryout line. The smell of cheese and pepperoni lay heavily in the air.

She wasn't sure what she was doing. Meeting a good friend's daughter, she told herself. Jamie couldn't get Doug telling her he loved her out of her head. But the fact remained, she would be leaving soon. A relationship would be complicated enough, let alone a long distance one. Sooner or later someone would have to move. His family was here, and she wasn't sure how much she was willing to give up. Or if she was ready at all.

"Over here," Doug directed Jamie toward their table. A passionate fluttering arose at the back of her neck as her eyes met Doug's.

"Hello, Ma'am," Haley burst out with joy.

"Hello, young lady. How was your trip to the lake?"

"It was fun, except the neighbor kid hit me in the nose with a rock. See, I have a bruise now. But it doesn't hurt anymore because my grandpa fixed it with a Rugrats Band-Aid, and he gave my teddy bear one because he had a bruise, too. I got to swim a lot and eat lots of stuff that my dad never lets me have," said Haley.

Jamie smiled as she looked at what had to be the cutest child she'd ever seen. Haley had a head full of perfect golden-blonde curls, and deep green eyes. She was wearing a cute skirt set with a matching pink bow in her hair. When Haley smiled, Jamie could see her upper right tooth was gone. She asked about it, and Haley explained it just fell out all by itself. She raised her hands up and shrugged to get her point across.

Jamie was pulled by the vitality zinging through the girl. She knew at that point her heart was gone, and this child had it.

"Are those presents for me?" Haley asked.

"Haley Marie, that's not polite," Doug said.

"Shame on me for making you wait so long," Jamie said. "I hope you like them." She pushed the gifts toward her so she could open them.

"Look, Daddy, a purse!" she said as she tore through the wrapping paper. "It's beautiful. I hope you're around for Christmas," Haley said.

Jamie could barely keep the laughter from her voice and grabbed Doug's hand to keep him quiet as he began to scold Haley for her comment. They devoured their pizza lost in conversation and light humor. Haley took turns sharing stories from summer, playing

with her new toys, and going a few rounds at the video games.

Jamie and Doug had decided if everything went well, Jamie would

stay at his house but sleep on the couch during the week. Haley was

staying at her grandparents for the weekend. Doug was insistent on

spending as much time with Jamie as possible.

"Are you spending the night tonight? We can have a slumber

party."

"If that's okay with you?"

"You can borrow my Barbie sleeping bag that my dad got me

for my birthday, but you have to give it back when you're done,"

Haley said, and Doug and Jamie both chuckled.

Doug held Jamie's hand while he was driving, and Haley

didn't seem to mind. Jamie wanted to be careful, though. She was,

after all, leaving soon and didn't want to mislead anyone. She

hadn't promised Doug anything nor had he asked. She also didn't

want to present something to Haley that wouldn't be there. The last

thing she wanted to do was make her feel like she was being left

behind again.

Even the others hadn't said a lot to her about leaving.

Everyone was just living in the day-to-day activities and not thinking

any further. Or at least not admitting it.

*   *   *

"God bless my daddy, Grandpa and Grandma, and all my

friends at school, and my new friend, Jamie." Haley prayed

alongside her bed. She then gave Doug a kiss and a hug, and told

her dad how much she loved him and climbed into bed. She

wrapped her arms around her doll and pulled her Barbie sheets over

her and closed her eyes.

Jamie watched from the hallway. Doug and Haley were

going to break her heart when she had to leave.

His arm around her waist, Doug led her to the living room.

She could fell his uneven breathing on her cheek as he held her

close. She settled back, enjoying the feel of his arms around her.

They stayed up and talked for hours, finally falling asleep in

each other's arms on the couch.

CHAPTER 14

"I just want to thank everyone for your help the past few weeks and for today," Jared announced to the group.

The pigs roasted and the kegs chilled, they lounged in the back and waited for the guests to arrive in a few hours. Tables sprawled out everywhere, decorated with streamers and balloons. Plastic lanterns, strung up on clotheslines, bounced around in the light breeze. Candy, bubbles, and other kids' toys were in baskets to keep the children entertained. The D.J. tested his equipment with various records. A two-tier chocolate cake filled with layers of Bavarian cream would be brought out once everyone arrived.

Alex and Cristal went in to change. Doug carried the gifts for Jamie out onto a table. Jared and Doug would be displaying a fireworks exhibit as their birthday gift to her.

He smiled as he watched Haley in full spirits in the yard playing with Remy.

Sam and Jared took an afternoon dip in the creek. Jamie watched them from her sunbathing spot on the porch. She noticed a comfort with them she hadn't seen before. Sam hadn't said anything, but it was obvious when they looked at each other that they had feelings for each other. Maybe they hadn't even realized it yet.

"There you are, I was wondering what happened to you, " Doug said, a disturbed look on his face.

"Is something wrong?"

"Still no leads. That bastard is out there somewhere…he could even be here today."

"It can't be anyone we'd know so well. Let's just enjoy the day," Jamie said.

Doug smiled and reached in for a kiss. They sat together on the porch swing until the guests began to arrive. Three pick-up trucks rolled in, bringing the other farmers who were involved in the clambake. They began to unload food and supplies. Doug wandered over to help while she ran up to change clothes.

After much thought, she chose a peach tank top and a khaki pair of shorts and decided to go barefoot. The country was starting to wear off on her. She piled her hair on top of her head and secured it with a peach barrette she found in Alex's room.

She was going to miss having the girls around to play sisters with: borrow clothes, tease each other, share secrets. She would have to make her visits more frequent.

She looked out the window and saw Doug's parents arrive and Haley run squealing with joy to the car to hug her grandparents. After one final look in the mirror, she headed downstairs. She'd be seeing people today she hadn't seen in years. As she walked outside, she realized it was the first time in a while she actually cared how she looked. For work, she had always made an effort, but that was about professionalism and image, not because she cared what others thought.

*   *   *

"Oh, look at you sweetheart, aren't you a sight for sore eyes. Come here and give us a hug. Honey, isn't she just a gem?" Doug's mom, Louise, said to her husband, Doug Sr., as they took turns with hugs.

"You look pretty good yourself," Jamie said to both of them. Doug's parents, high school sweethearts, were both in their mid-fifties. They still looked young, vibrant, and in love. How rare such a gift of long-lasting love was. They were the perfect example of happily-ever-after, something she hadn't believed in for a long time.

"How have you been, Jamie?" Doug's father asked. "I hope my son's looking after you."

"Won't let me out of his sight," she laughed.

"Come up to the house; there's some chairs in the shade," Doug said, leading the way.

"Look at my purse, Grandma, Jamie got it for me," Haley said. She began showing all the contents of the purse.

"Let's go sit in the shade, and you can show me everything. We'll let these two go socialize," Mrs. Miller said. "Go on, have fun, we'll keep this one occupied. And take this with you," she said. She pointed to the green bean casserole and a plate of fresh-cut homegrown tomatoes that currently rested in the backseat.

"Looks good," Doug said. He snatched a couple of tomatoes off the plate.

"Get your grubby hands out of there," Doug's mom said and smacked Doug's hand. Everyone laughed.

The farm was quickly filling up with townspeople as one car after another arrived. Sam, Jared, Alex, and Cristal were all making their rounds, greeting everyone and pointing them in the right direction for food and drinks. Appetizers filled bellies until dinnertime at 2 p.m. Jamie felt overwhelmed and a little overcrowded. It was exhausting repeating over and over again about her life with the niceties of small talk. She decided it was time for a beer. She helped herself to a tall glass of ice and poured a draft beer over it. She then plopped under a tree for a quick reprieve. Remy apparently agreed and galloped over to join her.

He'd been playing and running all day. The kids had worn him out. Some of the other guests had brought along a few of their dogs as well. Remy had chased them around his property. He seemed not to mind the company so much until a couple of dogs helped themselves to his food and water.

Jamie glanced around at all the activities while she petted Remy. Alex and Cristal were covered in dirt. They were playing volleyball in the homemade volleyball court. The Eagles record blared from the speakers, several groups were trying their hand at euchre, kids were engrossed in a game of tag, and a group of teenagers swam in the creek. Then there was Doug, along with several other men supervising, as the pigs roasted.

"Hey, there. You mind sharing that?" Sam pointed to her ice-cold glass of beer.

Jamie offered up her beer.

"Let's set out the food. I'm starving," Sam said.

The girls set out the plates, platters, and bowls of food. Jamie's mouth was watering just looking at the feast. There was every salad, potato, and dessert you could name. Meatballs, smoked salmon, dressing, homemade pies, brownies, the whole bit. They had the whole evening to munch. Plus leftovers were great for the morning's post-party clean up. It had been named years ago, probably because everyone came by to clean and the only way anyone had the strength was to start with a Bloody Mary and food. So, it became the follow-up party.

"You have got to taste this," Sam said, offering a deviled egg to Jamie.

Huge platters of cut pork were carried over. Jared rang the dinner bell. The local pastor said grace, and Jared and a few of the farmers added some words.

"We've had another blessed year. Thank you for coming. Enjoy yourself. Okay, get in line and dig in," Jared said.

Jamie overindulged. It was hard not to with every mouth-watering bite exploding with flavor. She had tried a little bit of everything, but the rhubarb pie she finished off with was the definite winner. Jamie grabbed a lawn chair and sat back to get some sun and watch the volleyball game. She intended to let her food settle before they started with her birthday festivities.

*   *   *

"Wake up, sleepy head," Doug shook her awake. "Sam needs you in the house."

She knew that every year the basement became a makeshift daycare for the kids to watch T.V. and sleep when it got late.

"I can't believe it's dark, how long have I been out?" Jamie asked, stretching her arms.

"About three hours. One minute you were watching us play and cheering us on, then I hadn't heard from you in a while. I look over, and you're out like a light."

"I guess a nap is what I needed."

"You can help round the kids up. Jared said he has a surprise for them at dark."

Jamie rounded up the kids, and Doug worked on bringing people closer to the DJ table.

"Everyone gather around, please," Doug said into the microphone. "Today is a double celebration, and we have a few surprises in store for everyone. Today is Jamie's twenty-eighth birthday. I'm very pleased that she's celebrating it here with all of us. I would appreciate if you all could join me in wishing her a happy birthday."

Alex carried the cake over to her, and Sam led the group through the happy birthday song.

Jamie made a wish and blew out the candles. Before she could even cut the cake, Sam pointed to the sky. Bursts of color consumed the night and rained, one bright drop after another.

Jamie looked around to see where the fireworks were coming from and saw Jared and Doug taking turns shooting displays in the air. Jamie sat back, all smiles. The event lasted about ten minutes. Doug then finished off his surprise with a square box wrapped neatly with a powdered blue bow. Doug had selected a gold bracelet with Jamie's name on it in diamonds.

"Doug, it's lovely, but it had to be awfully expensive. But I won't say you shouldn't have, because I'm glad you did," she said. She hugged him, and he helped secure the bracelet on her arm.

"You're welcome. When I saw it, I knew it was for you."

"Mine's next." Sam handed the package over to Jamie. There wasn't any paper on it, just a taped-up box. "Sorry, I'm not much on wrapping. I figured just ripping all the tape off would be enough work." Sam had gotten her a selection of various short and top sets. She couldn't help but smile at the bold colors and edgy styles.

"Thanks, Sam. Your message is clear. I'll start with the new fashion statement immediately. " She laughed with Sam.

Cristal was next and gave Jamie an antique silver-plated frame with a picture of Alex, Jamie, and Sam when they were kids.

"Where did you find this?"

"I asked Jared to hunt one down for me. It was roughed up a little, but with modern technology, it's good as new."

Jamie finished opening the rest of her gifts. She had an assortment of gift certificates, a CD, and some perfume.

The D.J. put on "It's Your Birthday," and Sam and Alex yanked her onto the dance floor.

"Let's get this party started," Sam laughed. Not long after the girls started dancing, others followed.

Doug watched Jamie dance from the sidelines. He sat with the other guys drinking beers.

"Got an extra one of those?" Sheriff Bobby Mason Jr. asked.

Doug tossed over another beer.

"We just got the kids settled downstairs in their sleeping bags. Now I can have some fun," Bobby said.

"I suppose you don't have any news?" Doug asked.

"Not really. We did get a missing person's report alert sent from Illinois. A couple never made it back from the festival. Their neighbor, who was watching their house and watering the plants, called the police when they didn't return Sunday. According to the neighbor, they needed a getaway, and they decided to spend the weekend here. I doubt there's any connection. I've had a few extra cars on duty keeping an eye on things. How about you, any other incidents?"

"Everything's been good, which worries me. He didn't just go away," Doug said.

"If this is the same guy from ten years ago, you're probably right. Watch out for yourselves," the sheriff said. "How much longer is Jamie in town?"

Doug didn't say anything, he just watched the girls dance, distracted by Jamie's graceful dancing.

Jared broke in and answered for him.

"Next Sunday is what her plane ticket says, the day after the reunion."

"I better get back to my wife. I'll keep you guys posted on any information," the sheriff said.

"Thanks, Bobby," Doug said. Jared nodded and waved as the sheriff walked off. "Decent turn out as usual," Jared said.

"Yup, decent," Doug said.

"Decent," Jared repeated.

"Something on your mind, Jared?"

"No, just making conversation is all."

"You've never been one to hold back, by all means, don't start now. Say what you need to say."

"I just don't want you to get your hopes up for something that may not be there, with Jamie I mean."

"I'm not a complete idiot, Jared. I know what's on the line. I'm enjoying today, and I'll worry about tomorrow, tomorrow. Backing off is not going to make it hurt any less. Besides, you've got a lot of room to be talking. I see how you look at Sam."

"Not even close to the same thing. Sure, she's hot and all, but that was a few dates back when we were kids years ago. We're just having fun hanging out. I know next week her bags will be packed, and she'll be sailing or whatever the hell she does on that boat," Jared said. They looked up when they heard the girls chanting, "Go! Go! Go!"

They were over by a makeshift bar doing shots.

"One thing's for sure, never a dull moment with them around," Jared said.

"I agree with you there," Doug said.

"Grab a glass and slam," Sam yelled at Jared. She then poured tequila in a glass along with seven-up and slammed it against the table. As it exploded in the glass, she handed it to Jared to guzzle. He warily downed the concoction, gasping for air and choking as he did so. Before he even had a chance to sit the glass down, Sam handed him another cup.

"What's in this?"

"Kessler, a little clam juice, and some other stuff mixed in. I don't know. Just drink it."

"What are we, back in college?" Jared asked.

Sam offered Doug a shot.

"I'll stick to my beer and laugh tomorrow," Doug said.

"Suit yourself," she said and gulped it down.

Several shots later, the girls headed out to the dance floor while the men began a game of poker.

A couple hours later, when a slow song began playing, Sam came over to steal Jared.

"Hey handsome, let's go for a round on the rug," she said, grabbing his hand, pulling him to the dance floor.

"I'm playing cards," Jared said.

"Go ahead; I'll take over for you," Jamie said.

"Thanks. I've lost enough money for one evening anyway."

People stumbled around, running into things, and became louder by the hour. It seemed that Doug was the only one not overindulging. Now Jared and Sam were on the dance floor, barely holding each other up and attempting to slobber all over each other.

It was close to two a.m., and Alex, Cristal, and most intelligent people had called it an evening. Left behind were the diehard partiers and card players. Doug had a lucky streak going on and had won quite a bit of money. He liked to think it was because of his skill, not that several of his opponents were inebriated. He'd

go one more round, then call it a night.

*   *   *

They didn't want to take him seriously. Well, he would

change that. He'd just wanted to take a peek and check out the

party. Then he'd seen Jamie with Doug. Doug had had the nerve to

kiss her. Touch her. Hold her. His anger was boiling. He had to let

them know he was around and watching.

A satanic smile spread across his thin lips as he envisioned

the look on their faces when they found it. Then maybe people

would start paying attention.

It didn't have to be this way. It didn't have to be so difficult.

It should be him out there dancing and laughing with Jamie.

He could envision his future in a few years with Jamie and

their children. Experiencing picnics and barbeques together as a

family. Just as other normal families did. They didn't need

outsiders. Just each other. He had to focus on his goal, to bring

Jamie home. Life would be so much better for her. He would make

her happy. Show her what true love was.

He was the only one that should be touching her. Once he had her, he would be making that very clear. Yes, when he was done with her, Jamie Donald would know where home is and how to act properly in her new surroundings. It was only a matter of time.

*   *   *

"How is it even possible to make such a mess?" Sam asked as she surveyed the disaster from the night before. There were piles of trash and debris scattered everywhere. Strewn about were half empty plates, smashed beer cans, knocked over tables and chairs, and crumpled articles of clothing. Someone had even managed to help themselves to several rolls of toilet paper and teepee'd the trees in the back. There were people passed out back in the garden. Apparently, the tents set up for that purpose two feet away were just too far.

Sam leaned against a table and shook her head. "My head is pounding. I've already barfed three times. What was I thinking?"

"Drink this." Doug handed her a Bloody Mary. "It might not go down smooth at first, but you'll start to feel better." He was also drinking one and eating a pork sandwich.

"I don't know if I can. How can you eat?" she asked in disgust.

"Unlike you and the rest of your posse, I didn't slam shots and mixed drinks. I'm surprised you're even functioning with everything you drank."

"Don't remind me. Please tell me I wasn't dancing on the table."

"I'm glad you remember," Doug smiled.

"Barely," Sam said. She took half a swallow of the Bloody Mary and ran to the bathroom.

Doug and Jared laughed and started folding tables and loading them on trucks.

"How are you today, big shooter?" Doug asked Jared.

"What are you talking about? I was sober last night," Jared said.

"Sober my ass. That's why you ran into a table and about broke your leg. Not to mention you slobbering all over Sam."

"We were just goofing around," Jared said.

"So how far did it go?"

"I woke up in her room. We were both somewhat dressed and too drunk to do anything. We think anyway. Just keep your big mouth shut. We chalked the evening up to alcohol, and we're past it."

"Tell it anyway you want. At least I admit I'm in love."

"Asshole. Just grab the end of the table and shut up, you're giving me a headache."

Doug smiled at the effect he had on Jared this morning.

Alex and Cristal handed out plates of food, leftovers from the night before. Jamie worked on the inside of the house cleaning and folding blankets that guests had used.

None of them felt particularly well this morning, but Sam was by far the worst. She had spent most of the morning in the bathroom.

"Why don't you lie down, and I'll get you an ice pack for your head, a couple of crackers, and some Tylenol," Alex said, mothering Sam.

Jamie handed Sam a mug.

"What is it?" Sam said, frowning down at the concoction.

"Green tea."

"You know I don't like tea."

"Trust me, this stuff works wonders. I haven't been sick in years. It'll knock that hangover right out of you. Or you can be miserable all day. It's up to you," Jamie said.

"All right," Sam said. She took a sip. "This stuff is disgusting. It'd better work. For all I know, you're just giving it to me to make me suffer more," Sam said.

"Not a bad idea, now that you mention it," Jamie said.

"It was *your* birthday. How come I was the one who did the celebrating?"

Jamie and Alex laughed.

They were just about finished in the late afternoon when Ken Mitchell, a local farmer, who went to burn all the trash in the barrels behind the barn yelled for Doug and Jared.

Doug and Jared came running.

"You'd better come take a look and fast."

Doug knew it was serious. Ken's face was pale and his eyes wide.

"What's going on?" Jared asked as he looked around the barrel and jumped back in shock. "Shit. That's not real, is it?"

"It's real," Doug said. He stared at the dead female body lying between the back of the barn and the trash barrels. A dead body was right in front of him. Rigor mortus had set in and the body lay very stiff on its left side. Half of the corpse was an off-gray ashen look. The other was pink, reddish, and blotchy. He reached to check for a pulse just to be sure. The skin was cold and wet. She was definitely dead.

"Who did this?" Doug said more to himself than anyone.

"Don't touch anything. I'll go call the sheriff," Jared said. He ran into the house to get the phone.

Meanwhile, Doug kept people from the area and instructed Ken to send everyone else home.

*   *   *

Doug knew the group was still in shock with the horror of what had happened. Bobby Mason Jr. and a couple of his men were finishing up. They removed the body, questioned everyone, collected and catalogued the necessary evidence. No identification or purse was found.

Bobby had called in the incident. Based on the photo he had from a missing person's report, the deceased was the missing woman from Chicago. She had been on their boat last weekend, which meant her husband was still missing.

The woman had been strangled to death. Black and blue marks were present on her wrists and ankles where she had been tied before her death. There was bruises and swelling where the murderer had roughed her up. The coroners' report said she'd been dead for at least a week and that she had probably been killed somewhere else and then her killer had moved her to behind the barn.

No one had ever been murdered in the town before. Everyone was pretty shaken. They could all be in real danger. Doug was especially nervous. He had a feeling this murderer was the same guy stalking Jamie.

Bright yellow crime scene tape had been wrapped around the garage and ten feet around the area. A local uniformed officer took statements from all the guests. The sheriff questioned Jared and Alex and suggested they do an inventory to see if anything was missing. The sheriff informed them a police car would be stationed out front as often as possible, and their residence would be part of their routine checks.

After the police left, no one really knew what to do.

Doug decided he'd better speak first and try and get a handle
on the situation.

"We need to be safe and hold our heads up high. This is
exactly what this person wants. For us to be frightened and upset.
We can't allow him to gain control."

"I know you're right, but I feel horrible," Alex said.

With everything that happened, they decided to stay in for
the evening. Doug drove into town and grabbed a bucket of chicken
and a couple of movies. Everyone in town had already heard about
the incident. It was unthinkable to believe that a murderer was
running loose in the community. He knew there would be a lot of
doors locked tonight, for the first time in years.

CHAPTER 15

Jamie was still in awe with the way the community came together in a crisis. The whole town had helped make the community safer with several new programs—giving rides to women who didn't have anyone with them, free self-defense classes, free home security systems being installed, even a special church service to bring the community together. Not at all like Chicago.

The girls hadn't ventured out much after all the excitement. Instead, they'd spent their time with each other. And Sam told them she'd decided to rent the Taylor cottage and stay in town for a while. She said it was for the winter. But Jamie wondered if Jared had anything to do with her decision. Sam would never admit it, but Jamie thought it did.

In the downtime, Jamie had finally checked in at work. Except for a few minor incidents, everything was running smoothly. Nothing someone else couldn't handle. She'd always thought the whole system would break down without her. Part of her was delighted everything was all right. Part of her was saddened by it. Her career was all she'd had for years. It made it seem okay if she was needed. Without that need, it didn't seem so important. In fact, her Chicago home seemed less and less exciting to her—the highways, the smog, the people everywhere. She didn't know where home was anymore.

All she knew was that she wanted to be part of Doug and Haley's life. Both had become important to her. It wouldn't be easy, but with vacations and weekends, she hoped they could agree on something. The thought of Doug in Chicago put a smile on her face. He would adjust. He was always one to go with the flow, but it would be an interesting experience. He had traveled on vacations, even seminars, but more often than not they were places like

Virginia and North Carolina. He'd even been to Alaska, but it

wasn't the same as Chicago.

She'd come up to her room to pack while the others watched

a video downstairs. She wanted to be ready Sunday so she could

head back early. She wanted time to readjust before going to work

on Monday. Besides she hated long, drawn out good-byes. She left

out her dress for the dance, a jogging suit, and an outfit for Sunday.

"What are you doing up here? You're missing a good movie

down there," Doug said. Then he noticed the open suitcases.

"Packing my clothes and thinking. I won't have any time

later with the girls' day at the spa tomorrow," Jamie said. Doug

looked angry so she tried to change the subject. "Can you believe

Alex and Cristal have never been to a day spa?"

Doug didn't take the bait. "So that's it? One more swing on

the dance floor tomorrow? Maybe a hop in the sack for old times,"

Doug said.

"I have a job. Did you think this would just go on forever?"

What the hell was she supposed to do? Anger seared through her.

"Were you expecting me to hang out in Alex's childhood bedroom for the rest of my life? Abandon my career?" she asked.

"I thought we'd talk about it first," Doug said.

"I've been honest with you from day one. I care for you, but I have a life to get back to." This was not going at all as she had hoped. She tried a different approach. "But I have a lot of vacation time built up, and we can rotate weekends." Jamie folded her pants and put them in her suitcase. When she didn't hear a response from Doug, she looked up. She softened her voice. "It's not the end of us, just the end of vacation."

"Weekends? That's not a relationship! Go back to your career, Jamie. Sorry to have kept you from it, here in Mayberry." Doug stormed out, slamming her door on his way. He marched down the stairs and out the front door.

Jamie sat on the bed and stared at the shut door. What had just happened?

"You okay in here?" Sam tapped on the door and entered, Alex and Cristal right behind.

The girls sat beside Jamie on the bed.

"I shouldn't have come here. Look what a mess I've made," Jamie said.

"That's crap, and you know it. Doug just doing what men do—having a hissy fit when things don't go their way. You have to do what's best for you." Sam grabbed a pillow for support as she lay back on the bed.

"That's just it, I don't know what is best for me."

"Go with your gut. If you're meant to be together, you will be," Alex said. Cristal reached over and took Alex's hand. They both knew about being together against all odds.

"Jared's out talking to him now," Cristal said.

"They'll do what they always do when they're pissed. Drink a few beers, throw a few darts, and bitch about us," Alex said, and Jamie smiled.

"Let's go to my room for a minute. I have something I want to show you," Alex said.

"I could use the distraction," Jamie said.

"What do you got in there?" Sam asked.

"Well, come see for yourself," Alex said.

The girls followed her down the hall. Jamie, Sam, and Cristal plopped down on the bed. Alex closed the door and began searching through items on the top shelf in her closet.

"Wow, do we have a secret mission here," Sam joked.

"Sort of. Do you remember this?" Alex asked, tossing a medium-sized box on the bed.

"You still have that after all these years?" Jamie asked.

"Have what?" Cristal asked.

Sam studied the box which was decorated with signatures.

"The Treasure Chest! Let's take a look," Sam said. She reached for the lid.

"Careful, this baby has ten years on it. Handle with care," Alex said.

"Here's your collection of key chains, Sam. 'Blondes don't have all the fun, just ask me!', 'Stop, I'm on fire'. My first place ribbons for 4-H. Look at these goofy pictures of us from our freshman year," Alex said.

The others continued to gently rifle through the contents.

"When I feel sad, lonely, or just miss you guys, I just go through the box. We're all in here," Alex said.

"Jamie, do you remember this?" Sam passed over a homemade invitation. It was for Jamie and Doug's wedding Jamie had been sure would come.

"Wow," Jamie said. The names were done in glitter. There was no exact date. Pictures of a bride and groom, doves, and a wedding ring had been cut out of a magazine and pasted on the cover. In blue water colors were the words 'Mr. and Mrs. Doug Miller.' She'd completely forgotten.

"That was a lifetime ago," Jamie said. Solemnly, she gently placed the invite back in the box. "We were kids. We didn't know any better."

"No one's asking you to explain or justify anything. It's just a box from school. Here, take a look at my old notebook," Alex said, handing Jamie a notebook paper with the words 'I Love Harry Fallman' written in a circular pattern over and over, filling up the whole page.

"Who's Harry Fallman?" Cristal asked, leaning over Alex's shoulder to see the paper.

"I heard he moved to Michigan, sells insurance now," Alex said. "No one you need to worry about," she leaned over and kissed

Cristal lightly. "The moral of the story, Jamie, is that I'm obviously not spending my days pining over him."

"How about you, Sam?" Jamie asked.

"Oh, no. I think we've had as much of the hope chest as we can manage for one day," Sam said, fastening the lid back in place. "Enough of this sentimental shit for a day. Can we finish our movie, please?" Sam asked.

*   *   *

"Could you use some company?" Jared asked. Doug was shooting darts.

"It's your garage. Do what you want," Doug said.

Jared walked in and leaned against his desk, which was cluttered with papers and farmer almanacs.

"Anything I can do?"

"You might as well grab me a Miller out of the fridge," he said.

"Want to tell me what's got you so fired up?" Jared asked and handed over the beer.

"I suppose you already know."

"Thought you might want to get it out of your system."

"Don't think that's ever going to happen. Up for a game?"
Doug handed him the darts.

"Sure, since you ruined my movie." Jared took the darts and
began his turn. "I take it she's leaving Sunday as planned, and
you're not thrilled about it?"

"Nothing I didn't know was going to happen in the back of
my head. I was just wishing for something else. I wasn't ready to
see her packing up her stuff and talking about leaving. One minute
we're watching a movie, the next thing I know, she's gone. Just like
the last time." Jared nodded.

"One minute she needs me. The next she's ready to go
home."

Jared threw another dart and stayed silent.

"Go ahead," Doug said. "Say it."

"Did she ever say she was leaving you?"

Jared went and retrieved his darts and watched Doug aim.

"What are you getting at?" Doug asked.

"She has a job, right?"

"Yeah."

"A career more like it. A place to live, friends, commitments, even some memories there?"

"Yeah, probably."

"So for the last ten years that's been her home."

"Is this going somewhere?"

"Jamie's not leaving you. She's going back to the only home she's had for years. And you want her to just give all that up so she can hang out here with you? And what exactly are you giving up?"

"When the hell did you become so sensitive to women's needs?" Doug asked.

"Hey, I have a sister," Jared said.

"I just want to be with her. For the rest of my life."

"It took ten years for her to come back. It's gonna take more than four weeks to change her whole life."

"So, what's your suggestion, drop her off at the airport and wave good-bye?" Doug said.

"Would it kill you to visit her in Chicago on the weekends? Have you ever thought that if you love her enough, you might have to make some sacrifices too?"

"I'm not that selfless of a guy. I want her here."

"Have you ever considered you moving there? Chicago can't be all bad. You'll have the Bears, Cubs, and the White Sox in your backyard. Not much to complain about there," Jared said.

"Okay, thanks Dear Abby," Doug said.

"Yeah, maybe I'll take on a second job. I'm pretty good, aren't I?" Jared grinned.

"How much of that advice did you get from Alex?"

"All of it. Except for the sports stuff—that was mine." Jared downed the rest of his beer. "I'm going back inside to watch my movie, you coming?"

"Yeah, I am."

CHAPTER 16

"I feel like Jell-O," Alex sighed, sprawled out on a massage table.

"Every thirty days is mandatory to keep your sanity," Sam said.

"This is sensational. I can barely move," Cristal said.

"I'm glad you're enjoying yourselves," Jamie said.

"So what happened when you and Doug were talking in the dining room? You weren't in there very long," Sam asked. Her massage therapist kneaded the tension out of her shoulders.

"He apologized for walking out and blowing up. I apologized. We're gonna rotate weekends, and I'll visit for the holidays."

"Really? With the way you two look at each other, I kind of thought you'd stay," Cristal said.

"My focus is in marketing. What am I going to do here? Sell pigs for a living?"

They enjoyed the rest of their massages and then went to get dressed.

"What's next?" Alex asked.

"God Alex, I don't know okay," Jamie said. She was tired of the twenty questions.

"I meant today. At the spa."

"Sorry," Jamie said. "I'm just a mess right now. Ignore me..."

"While we're getting our hair done, Cindy's going to paint our nails and Sherry will do our eyebrows," Sam said. "I want to try the new two-minute spray-on tan. I thought we'd select some products to take with us and then lunch."

Alex looked up in alarm.

"Eyebrows! No one said anything about that. You must be out of your mind if you think I'm letting, actually paying, someone to rip hair off my face with hot wax."

"You wimp. You have to get with the times. You've got the unibrow going there. Besides, I already paid for it," Sam said.

"You should've saved your money."

"Well, if you're that big of a baby…" Jamie said, baiting her friend.

"I just don't see the point." Alex turned to Cristal. "You're awful quiet over here. Are you going to submit yourself to this torture?"

"Let's give it a try," Cristal said.

"They can also do your lip and…"

"No way," Alex interjected before Jamie could finish. "You get the eyebrows, and that's it. My *lip* stays blissfully unwaxed!"

Jamie laughed.

"If I knew this was part of the plan, I would've gone golfing with the guys," Alex said. She gripped her nails into the chair's upholstery as the technician slabbed on hot wax. Then a few seconds later, she put on some cloth and yanked it off. "Son of a bitch, that hurt! You do this every six weeks? For what?"

"You get used to it," the technician rubbed on some aloe to ease the swelling.

"What do you think?" Cristal asked Alex as she posed for her, modeling off her new hairstyle, brows, and nails.

"You're in a cheery mood for just having hair ripped out," Alex said.

"You're all set," the technician said as she turned her chair around for Alex to review the finished product in the mirror. "The red swelling will go away in an hour or so."

"You look hot baby; we all do. We're gonna set our reunion on fire when we walk in tonight," Sam said.

"Do you have tequila in that soft drink or something?" Alex asked.

"No, honey. Feeling sexy and ready to kick up my heels tonight. That's what we're all here for, right? Let's grab a bite to eat," Sam said.

*   *   *

"Let's go already. We're going to be late. For God's sake, you think you were getting married with all the fuss," Jared yelled up the stairs.

"Relax, you know how women are. We've got time," Doug said.

"We're ready," Alex shouted.

The guys turned around and stopped dead in their tracks as the girls approached, Alex and Cristal first, then Sam and Jamie last.

Jared could barely even recognize the four women strutting down the stairs. Alex had her hair cut and angled toward her face. It was the first time he'd ever seen her wear lipstick. He had to admit, for his sister, she looked terrific. Cristal didn't look half bad either. What he wasn't prepared for was Sam. Her long, curly hair ran wild with just a hint of glitter. Her bronzed skin stood out against a white sleeveless dress.

"Wow," he whispered.

Doug's gaze was riveted on Jamie's face. Jamie's hair was pulled back, and her neck look graceful and long. How he wanted to place his lips right there. The blue dress she wore accented her curvaceous body. She looked radiant.

"Excuse me, I'm looking for my sister and her goofy-looking friends," Jared said.

"Very funny," Alex said.

"Just rattling your chain. All of you look hot. Very hot. Except you, Alex. You look nice."

"Gee, thanks."

"Every guy in that place is gonna have his tongue hanging out," Doug said.

Jamie felt a ripple of excitement run through her when she locked eyes with Doug. She was entirely caught up in her own emotions. It was too easy to get lost in the way Doug looked at her.

Sam wrapped her arm around Jared's and led him out the door.

"You two don't look so bad yourselves," Alex said to the guys.

"I didn't know you had hair under all those hats you wear," Sam said. "I see you even found the brush."

*   *   *

Shrimp, meatballs, stuffed mushrooms, freshly cut fruits, and vegetables neatly adorned the makeshift bar, where they had been directed after registration. Tropical drinks with umbrella stirrers stood in colorful rows.

The air felt warm and dry against Jamie's skin. The sun had begun its descent. It colored the night with a pleasant mixture of yellow and oranges. The sky would be crowded with glimmers of light splashed against the dark.

The band bellowed out tunes and made her feel like dancing. She walked lightly on the platform over the sand near the calm, nearly smooth lake. Sliver and gold lights wrapped themselves around the trees and poles and among the tents set up for the steak and lobster buffet.

How romantic, she thought as she moved through the bouquets of mixed flowers scattered about.

Jamie talked with former classmates while Doug went to get drinks. She could hardly maintain the proper interest. She couldn't stop thinking about Doug.

Doug finally showed up with two glasses of Merlot. "Long line. You ready for dinner?"

"I'm always ready for food. Lead the way," Sam said, sneaking up behind them.

The aroma of meat and melted butter filled the dinner tent. Jamie found her seating tag and looked furtively at the others perched by the dinnerware. She had Cristal at her table, along with two gentlemen who were married to women from school. Both were polite and spoke as needed, yet kept to themselves. Just as Jamie preferred.

*   *   *

"May I have this dance, Jamie?" Doug asked.

She nodded and rose. She put her head on Doug's shoulder and allowed herself to listen to the music as she glanced out at the lake.

She was impressed with the reunion committee and the work they had done with the set-up, decorations, and the dance.

Everything worked together perfectly. It was a night filled with happiness and memories. What more could she possibly ask for?

"Thank you for escorting with me," Jamie said and gave him a gentle kiss on the lips.

They continued dancing. When the song came to an end, Doug asked, "Would you like to accompany me for a stroll along the shore?"

"I would."

They hurried away from the others and discarded their shoes in the sand to feel the cool water splash against their feet.

Doug turned around and looked directly at her.

"I know I can't expect you to make all the sacrifices in order for us to be together. You're right, we can't live like we are now on vacation."

"Doug, you don't have to…"

"I've been rehearsing this speech all day," Doug said with a smile, "and I'm going to say it."

"Go ahead."

"I'm complete when I'm with you. I want to wake up every morning, and be able to look over into the eyes of my soul mate.

I'm willing to make adjustments to be with you." Doug got down on one knee in the sand. "Will you marry me?" He reached in his pocket for the ring and slipped it on Jamie's finger.

Tears slid down her cheeks as she admired the ring, and she stared at it wordlessly. The jewel was white gold and had one amazing diamond in the center with several circling around it in a shape of a flower. It was the most amazing piece of jewelry she'd ever seen.

She hadn't expected this. Her heart raced, and her hands shook as she swiped the tears from her face. A thousand thoughts went spinning through her head.

"Wow, I didn't expect…" Jamie stopped when she saw someone running towards them. He was waving his hands in the air, yelling something at them that she couldn't make out.

"Emergency! Doug, come…" was all she understood.

"What?" Doug yelled. "What's wrong?"

"Doug, it's your daughter; there's a phone call on hold in the lobby. Your daughter's been taken!"

The color suddenly drained from Doug's face.

"Go, go. I'll gather our shoes and be right behind you," she said.

"God, please let her be okay." Doug and the messenger ran full speed toward the office.

Jamie looked up to the sky, closed her eyes, and said a prayer for Haley and Doug.

She bent over to pick up the shoes. The sharp pain against the back of her head knocked the wind out of her. Before she could gain her balance and see what hit her, she felt another one. She couldn't stay on her feet, and she fell helplessly into the enveloping darkness.

*   *   *

Doug sped like a maniac all the way home. His thoughts were only on the safety of his daughter. The call was a tape recording of a man, and it only said that he had Haley. Doug was to report home immediately and wait for further instruction. What in the hell was happening in this once quiet and safe town?

He raced into the house and burst through the front door. He saw his mom sitting on the couch reading a magazine. His dad was on the recliner watching the news. They both looked up at him like he'd lost his mind.

"What happened? Where the hell is Haley?" he screamed.

"Doug, what is wrong with you?" his mom said.

"Where is Haley? Mom, where is she?" Doug said. He almost choked on his fear.

"She's in her room sleeping."

Doug darted upstairs, pushed open her door, threw back the sheets, and saw his sweet little girl tucked away in her bed, cuddled next to her teddy bear as always.

"Oh, thank God," he whispered. "Thank God." Careful not to wake her up, he bent down and gave her a soft kiss on her forehead.

Shaken, he went back downstairs and fell against the couch in exhaustion. Hoarsely, he explained to his parents about the phone call he had received.

"No wonder you came barreling in the door like a half-crazed lunatic," his mom said.

"What would possess someone to play such an evil prank?" his dad asked.

"I don't know. I'm just relieved it was a prank. I've never felt so much pain in my entire life as I have for the last twenty minutes."

"You didn't recognize the voice?" Doug's dad asked.

"No, it was taped, and the voice was skewed. At the time that wasn't my top priority."

"Of course, sweetheart. Where's Jamie?" his mom asked.

Jamie. His breath caught in his throat, and the queasy feeling came rushing back. It was never Haley he was after. It was Jamie.

"I left her alone on the beach. Keep an eye on Haley and lock all the doors."

Please be wrong, he prayed. He tried to hold back his fear as he ran out the door.

*   *   *

"Where's Jamie?" Doug asked. He had found Jared, Alex, Sam, and Cristal. He hadn't found Jamie.

"She was with you. What happened? Where's Haley?" Jared asked.

"It wasn't Haley," Doug said. He could barely get out the words. His panic rose in his throat. "She was home sleeping. I left

Jamie on the beach. She was going to gather our things–he took her! How could I be so stupid? I could've waited a few seconds for her."

"We don't know that she was taken," Jared said. "We'll look around here and see if anyone has seen her. Let's meet back here in ten minutes."

*   *   *

They had looked everywhere, and there was no sign of Jamie. Only footprints on the sand.

Both his and Jamie's shoes were still where they left them. One set of footprints led to the end of the beach and then disappeared into the water. The steps were too large to be Jamie's. The imprints looked like that of a boot. There were also partial marks that looked like someone had been dragged to a big log where the prints ended. The sheriff had arrived, and they were recounting the evening's events and scanning the area for clues. Doug's mind continued to race as he searched for a plausible explanation.

"Don't worry. We'll find her," Jared said.

"Technically, a person isn't missing for twenty four hours," the sheriff said. "In this situation, I think we have enough reason to be concerned. I suggest you all go home and stay close to the phone.

If I have any more questions or leads, I'll call. I'll get every car I have out on the road and radio into the city for some extra help. Write down every single thing you each talked about and did with her in the last four weeks. Try and remember your surroundings, people, places, anyone looking a little too long. It's usually the minute details that break a case."

"Shouldn't we be out looking for her?"

"We don't need anyone else to turn up missing. I'll call if there's anything you can do. I've got them back at the office running a list of all boats registered in the area."

"Didn't you say the woman found dead at the farm was reported missing and was supposed to be here on a boat trip?" Doug asked, his mind circling in all directions.

"We're inquiring into that. We should have the file and description of the boat first thing in the morning."

"I know you'll do everything you can, Bobby," Doug said.

*   *   *

Doug was in shock. He could barely hear his friends' voices.

"I've done my list, and I don't see anything useful on here. The farm, ice cream, the creep at the festival no one saw, all regulars, no one unusual. Maybe we should all switch lists to review," Alex said.

"That's not a bad idea, and we can ask each other questions," Sam said.

"Doug, what do you think?" Jared asked.

Doug looked up from his list. "I'm sorry, what did you say?" Both fear and anger distracted him.

By 3 a.m., after hours of pouring over notes, they weren't getting any nearer to answers. The phone hadn't rung once. Every person they could think of had been called and notified, but asked to only call if they had any information. It was essential to keep the line open. Doug had hoped Jamie had her cell phone with her. She didn't. It was in her room.

Jared devised a sleeping schedule so someone was always awake, and everyone could get a couple hours rest.

"I can't believe I let this happen to her," Doug said, the sense of guilt weighing on him. "I will find her."

He did not sleep that night.

CHAPTER 17

Jamie awoke with a swollen head and horrid pain. She struggled to gain consciousness. She was lying on an unfamiliar mattress, her hands and legs bound. He had hit her. He had taken her here. Panic set in, and her breathing became ragged. Her heart was hammered. Was he in the house with her?

Her chest tightened, and she began to gasp for air. She had

to gain control.

Calm down. Take a few deep breaths. Count to ten.

She wasn't a naïve teenager anymore. She would get out.

She studied the room for any possible escape and anything that could

be used as a makeshift weapon if she was able to break free.

A fire burned in the fireplace, unusual for the middle of

August, but nothing about this situation was normal.

There was only one window. If she leaned over just enough,

she could peak outside. It was dawn outside. The only door was to

the right of her. Three deadbolts locked her in. Only a key would

get her out.

The aroma of something cooking floated in the air. Jamie

hated to admit it, but it actually smelled edible. She was hungry.

She was in the bedroom of a cabin. There were no sheets,

and the mattresses were damp and stained, creating a musty pungent

odor that pierced into the air. Across the room was a three-legged

broken end table and a dresser with a missing drawer. A desk in the

corner was cluttered with papers. A dismal attempt had been made at decorating the unkempt room with seashells—a mix of yellow-stained pictures and broken trinkets. Her favorite.

The birds chirped along with the hum of bees and cicadas. I must be in the woods again, she thought. She began to review the first tormenting experience as much as possible and the mistakes she had made. She would not make the same mistakes this time.

Would he kill her? She couldn't allow it to escalate to that point. She had to be ready to escape as soon as an opportunity presented itself. She felt dizzy, and her vision blurred momentarily. Her head throbbed.

She attempted to free herself from the ropes to no avail. Both her hands and legs were tight and unmovable.

She wondered if they were looking for her. Doug, I'm here, she tried to send out her thoughts to him. Had this man taken Haley too? She prayed that Haley was safe.

She heard footsteps approaching. Raw fear surfaced again. Should she pretend she was still sleeping? She decided to face her attacker. She heard each bolt snap back into place.

"I see you're awake, my dear. I made your favorite breakfast." His voice was the same one from years ago. "We have bacon, ham, tomato and cheese omelet with a side of biscuits and gravy." He had a tray with him.

"I also brought a few magazines I thought you would enjoy and a couple of blankets, blue flannel, your favorite. Hopefully these favorites will make you feel at home and more comfortable. I also have some clothes for you in the closet. Size six, right?"

She stared at him. It was the man who had raped her. The man from the bar.

"I've studied you very carefully," he said.

She shivered unintentionally. He had been watching her.

"I'm going to untie your hands so you can eat. I have a fresh bowl of soap and water and a towel so you can clean up."

Jamie knew this was her chance. She must have shown hope on her face, because her attacker leaned in close to her face.

"If you try anything, I will have to punish you."

As he bent to untie her hands, he whispered into her ear, "There's no way out. Even if you managed to get out, you're a long way from anyone. Not to mention the added traps you'll have to avoid."

He laughed with glee at his cleverness. He had thought of everything this time.

"You'll see, my love. You belong with me. This is *our* reunion. Fitting that I took you to your new life on the night of our ten-year class reunion."

His voice went cold, his eyes flat and hard.

"I will be back in precisely thirty minutes. I expect you to be fed, dressed, and ready. You will do as I say."

"What do you want from me?" He stood silent and calm. "Answer me, damn it! Fucking answer me, you bastard!" she yelled through a thick layer of tears.

"I would suggest you save your threats. You're really not in a position to execute them." His voice was absolutely emotionless, and it chilled her.

With that, he walked out and bolted the door behind him. She then saw that the windows had bars on them. Funny, she hadn't even noticed them with her previous once-over of the area. I have to be more careful. Think clearly. See clearly.

Clouds hung thick in the sky creating sudden darkness and the promise that a storm would soon be here. She concentrated on the moment at hand as she rubbed the never-ending stream of tears

from her eyes. Crying wasn't going to help, but she couldn't stop.

Think. She had to think.

She began to dress and then stopped with a sudden

realization. He had said *our class reunion.* She had thought her

rapist had been much older. But at the time, her vision had been

skewed by fear and mud and blood. The man who had raped her ten

years ago had attended her high school.

She sat down and ate the food while she thought of anyone

who might have worn glasses with dark, greasy hair in high school.

The food was actually good, but her erratic nerves made it difficult

to eat. She thought of needing to escape and forced herself to eat

more. She needed her strength.

Then she combed her hair and secured it back in a ponytail.

Her mind was clouded by confusion and fear. She flipped aimlessly

through one of the magazines and tried to put this man with someone

who she might have known in high school.

That's when it dawned on her. She knew who he was. Ernie

Stanton, a loner in school. He was always picked on, beat up on and

the butt of mean practical jokes. She didn't get it though. Jamie was one of the few people who went out of her way to be nice. That's the way she was raised. She felt sorry for him and made a valid effort to be his friend. She often sat next to him at lunch, chose him for a partner when no one else would, helped him study, and she stepped in to keep people from teasing him. But even then, he had given her the creeps.

Time hadn't treated him well. His face was weather-beaten and his hands calloused, which made him appear years older than his age. His teeth were crooked and stained.

She felt despair then. No one would remember him. No one would ever suspect Ernie. It would be a long time before she would be rescued. She would have to go along with Ernie and his deranged fantasy. He was a rapist and a murderer, and she had to stay alive. She gazed at the ring on her finger and remembered Doug proposing to her. She never had a chance to answer him.

She heard the deadbolts being unlocked. He was here again. She inhaled a big gulp of air to prepare herself. She wouldn't be scared. She racked her brain for any detail she could remember about him that might help her get out of here.

"I see you followed my instructions. You're a good girl. You look respectable now, more suitable then this slutty dress you wore here." He grabbed the dress she had worn and threw it in the fire. "I see you ate all your breakfast. You're such a good, good girl." He leaned in and kissed her on the lips. She tried hard not to vomit or push him away.

He noticed the ring on her finger and pulled it off. "You won't be needing this anymore, either." Ernie placed it in his pocket. He then removed two plain gold bands from his shirt pocket. He placed one on his finger and the other on Jamie's. The ring slid around her finger, leaving behind a rust-colored residue.

He ran his bony fingers through her hair. Then proceeded to brush his hand against her face. She let out a strangled cry by accident. She knew it would displease him. But his touch was so revolting, she couldn't stop herself.

"That's okay, I can be patient. We'll have plenty of time to get to know each other. No one will be marrying you except me. I took the liberty of planning the whole occasion. A small wedding, just the two of us." He seemed very pleased with himself.

"But I was kind to you!" Jamie protested.

"I see you're starting to remember me. You defended me. That's how I first knew we were meant to be together. I knew right away you loved me. I've watched and studied you since the day you walked me home from first grade. We understood each other. Doug doesn't have that kind of connection with you."

"I was helping you because it was the right thing to do. You think I want this?" she asked. When he didn't answer, she became so frustrated. She began to yell at him. "No woman wants to be violated, tied up, threatened! That's not love!"

"Just shut up, you bitch!" Ernie slapped her hard across the face. She saw then that there was no reasoning with him. "I know what you want and what you need. You'll do as you're told, or you'll end up just like the woman you found behind the barn. All whores who need guidance from men." His nostrils flared with fury. He retied her hands hastily, then exited, slamming the door behind him.

Where was Haley? She had to find out if Haley was in the house. Jamie fought back the tears as the pressure of it all weighed on her. Panic welled in her throat. In his mind, they were a couple, and she loved him.

Her hands bled from the rubbing of the ropes, and she tried to fight the intense nausea and desolation that suddenly swept over her.

Fuck this asshole, she thought, and pulled and yanked in every direction.

"Let me out of here, you asshole!" she screamed through angry tears as loudly as she could until her throat was raw with unuttered shouts and protests. A heaviness centered in her chest, and she swallowed the despair in her throat. The whole nightmare was senselessly and sickeningly familiar. There was nothing left in her. Her forearms were red and sore, and she wept silently. Then she got down on her knees, cupped her trembling hands together, bowed her head and prayed for help.

*   *   *

"I can't just sit here anymore and do nothing. I'm going to the station and see what they've got so far," Doug said. He snatched his keys and stomped for the door.

"I'll ride along," Jared said. "If you get any calls or think of anything, call us there."

Alex nodded as the three girls drank their coffee and reviewed for the sixth time the circumstances from the past few weeks.

Sam suddenly jumped up from the table.

"Instead of dissecting every person we've talked to and every place we've gone to, what we should be doing is analyzing Jamie's account of the last attack she told us about."

"Okay," Alex said. "Good idea."

"She was originally attacked when she was going to the old clubhouse."

"Yeah, but that's been torn down for years."

"I know, but remember her account of that day. He knew the layout of the woods," Sam said.

"And right when the clubhouse was torn down, there was also a cabin out there that burned to the ground," Alex continued.

Cristal jumped in. "I know the spot you're talking about. There's a new one built. It's about five miles back from the public path. There's a guy who lives there that comes into town every day for supplies. Doesn't talk to anyone and heads back out, a real loner, kind of creepy…"

Alex got up and started pacing. "He went to school with us. Sam, what was his name?"

"Who?" Sam asked.

"He followed Jamie around like a puppy dog. Grab me the yearbook from the bookshelf. A nerdy-looking character." Alex flipped through the yearbook. "Ernie, Ernie Stanton," Alex said, pointing to the picture.

"But she was the only one who treated him with any kindness," Sam said. "It couldn't possibly be him."

"I've always had a bad feeling about that guy. Who else would know the woods so well?"

Sam conceded. "Let's go."

"I know where that cabin is built," Cristal said.

"Sam, you drive. I want to review the map on the way out there." Alex grabbed a rifle out of Jared's gun cabinet and a couple of boxes of shells and threw them in the truck.

"What are you gonna do with those?" Sam asked.

"I'm gonna use them if I need to. All those years of clay target practice may come in handy after all."

"This is great and all she-ra, but don't you think we should stop at the station and get backup?" Cristal asked. "Besides, what if we're wrong?" She tossed Alex the phone to call the station.

"If we're wrong, we'll just say we're sorry to have disturbed him and go back to the drawing board. But I don't think we are," Sam said.

Alex got through to Jared and explained their theory, and where the cabin was located. Jared warned the girls to stay put until they got there. The signal cut out as they sped down a narrow dirt path surrounded by a thick wall of trees.

"What did he say?" Cristal asked.

Sam drove around loose limbs and slowed down as rain set in and pelted heavily against the windshield. Thunder and lightning were not too far behind them, and by the looks of the sky, it was going to get worse.

"To stay put until they get here."

"No way," Sam said. "I couldn't live with myself if ten minutes would have made the difference between us finding her alive and finding her dead."

"I can't take that chance either," Alex said.

They all nodded in agreement. They would go on.

CHAPTER 18

Jamie's whole body was engulfed in tides of weariness and despair. She was so tired her nerves throbbed. She had spent the better part of the morning drifting into fits of sleep.

Startled, she flinched when she heard the door creek open. Ernie entered the room and began to untie her. He had on a tight gray suit with a tattered green bow tie and a ruffled white shirt. In any other situation, she would've found it humorous.

"Put this on," he said. He held out a frilly, shabby wedding gown and veil.

"What?" she asked. Sheer fright swept through her.

"Don't be difficult. The preacher will be ready in ten minutes. I expect you to be ready as well."

She began to protest but thought better of it. Instead, she thought of a way to find out if Haley was really there.

"Is that why you took Haley? To be the flower girl?"

"Took who? Oh that?" Ernie grinned. "Sweet heart. I had to get you alone. I never even thought about needing a flower girl. Should've really taken her," he mumbled. "Do you want one?"

"No, no. The priest is enough." Jamie breathed a sigh of relief. It was just her he wanted then.

Her relief was only momentary.

"Put it on now," he ordered.

She waited for him to leave and then she realized. He wanted to watch her.

Fury almost choked her as she tried hard to fight back the tears that slowly made their way down her cheeks.

She tried stalling for time. "You can't force someone like this. You can't force me to—"

He grabbed a pile of her hair and balled it up in his fist. Then he yanked her head back, and his eyes grew dark when he faced her.

"Don't forget what I'm capable of. You will marry me. You will, or I will kill everyone you know until you do, starting with your lover boy." He jerked her head, and she nodded. "Now get dressed. I have a surprise for you," he said.

Terrified by his threats and overcome with panic, she did as he demanded and slipped on the dress. The single-layered silk gown and veil was covered with thick-threaded material in some attempt of a design. It hung on her, two sizes too big. The veil was attached to a handmade crown.

She had no choice. She would have to marry him and hope for escape.

Ernie retied her hands, blindfolded her, and led her out of the cabin. He pushed her along, tightening his grip on her arm. Jamie stumbled several times concentrating on every step. Where was he leading her? She knew they were outside, and rain blew against her. He must've had an umbrella above her because her hair wasn't getting wet. She tried in vain to see through the fabric of the blindfold.

After a few minutes, he unwrapped the blindfold. All she could see were white dots. It took several blinks to get her eyes into focus. They were standing at the edge of a small dock in front of a boat. On the side, 'Chicago, Illinois' was painted in red. No houses were in sight, no vehicles, and certainly no help. Only endless miles

of water. Anxiety burned in her belly when she realized how slim

her chances were of getting away.

"Do you like your surprise?" Ernie asked.

She could not speak. This was probably the boat of the

woman he had killed. How could he have thought she would

appreciate a stolen boat that was owned by someone he had

murdered?

She just nodded slowly. Then, he pressed a gun up to her

back and shoved her onto the boat.

She stepped shakily into the boat, trying to keep her balance

with Ernie repeatedly thrusting her forward. In front of her, a priest

was tied to a chair. He struggled to escape, his eyes wide with panic.

She smelled something rancid and looked over. On the floor in the

corner was a dead man, his body stiff, blotchy, and swollen with

patches of redness. Her husband, she thought. Both dead.

Horror clutched her throat, making the act of inhaling a

single breath difficult. She didn't want to die. She couldn't give in

to him. She had to think.

He had placed what looked like bunches of weeds in plastic cups. Next to them, an old blue record player whirred out old jazz tunes. Ashtrays overflowed with cigarette butts, empty soda cans and food wrappers lay scattered about the boat. The once-treasured boat was now a broken toy for a madman.

She saw out of the corner of her that Ernie was distracted by the priest's struggles to escape. She elbowed Ernie with all her might and cracked him in the ribs. Ernie winced over in pain. She swung around and kneed him in the groin. The pain brought him to his knees. Jamie kicked at him again.

Not quick enough. Ernie grabbed her leg before it hit him and pulled her down to the ground with him. The pain she had inflicted only seemed to fuel his anger. He let out a howling screech that echoed through the woods. He grabbed his pistol from the floor where he'd dropped it in pain and clubbed her face with the butt end. Her head cracked back.

"A little more feisty than I remember. You want it rough my love, that's fine by me. But, unless you want the death of a priest on your conscience, I suggest you stop struggling," Ernie said. He positioned himself and Jamie in front of the priest, his gun poised in his right hand. "Keep it short."

"Do you take this woman to be your lawfully wedded wife, to have and to hold until death do you part?" the priest asked Ernie.

"I do," Ernie said. He reached out for Jamie's hand. Jamie almost gagged in disgust.

"Do you take this man to be your husband?"

Jamie swallowed the sob that rose in her throat.

Suddenly, a loud crash came from above.

"Ah, guests for the wedding. Please come in, have a seat," Ernie pointed his gun at Sam, Alex, and Cristal who had tried unsuccessfully to sneak onto the boat.

"So much for the art of surprise!" Sam said with a scowl towards Alex.

"I slipped, okay?" Alex said.

"You can leave the rifle there on the floor. That is if you want to live."

Alex put the rifle on the floor.

"If I would have known we'd have such a large turnout for the wedding, I would've gotten a yacht," Ernie said.

*   *   *

"Where the hell are they? I told them to stay put," Jared said. When Doug and Jared had arrived with the sheriff, they searched the cabin but had found no one.

But what they had found made them all shudder. The cabin served as a shrine to Jamie. The room was filled with her favorites, cracked and broken shells, magazine cutouts of shells yellowing around the edges, pictures of her life over the past few weeks on the small metal kitchen table.

At that point, they realized what they were up against. A madman.

He was obsessed with Jamie. It was quite apparent that she was his world. Doug's fear for her deepened with this new knowledge.

Doug focused. His only thoughts were on how he would stop this man.

They walked outside almost in a daze. The evil was palpable.

Then Doug saw a splash of white in the distance against the green of the trees. "It looks like there's a boat out there on the lake."

Doug motioned through the trees. Then Doug thought back to the footprints on the beach where they had last seen Jamie.

"Could be the one that couple from Chicago had," the sheriff said.

"He could have used the boat to bring Jamie here," Jared said, catching on.

"They could be there now." Doug began running toward the boat.

"Hold on, Doug, backup's on the way," the sheriff said. "We don't know the situation. If he has the girls, he'll be expecting us too. We need to split up and cover all directions. We don't want anyone getting hurt."

*   *   *

"Do you take this man to be your lawfully wedded husband, to have and to hold, until death do you part?"

Jamie could not bring herself to say the words. Ernie raised the gun at the priest and finally she spoke.

"Yes," she whimpered. There were too many lives at stake. She couldn't take any chances.

"You may kiss the bride."

"Come here, my dear." He grabbed her hair so she could not escape and shoved his tongue down her throat.

She had to fight back the urge to throw up as he slobbered all over her.

Sam sat on the floor, both Alex and Cristal in front of her to keep Ernie from seeing. As Ernie kissed Jamie, Sam slowly reached for the revolver she had in the back of her pants.

"Wasn't that lovely?" he said finally coming up for air. "After I dispose of everyone, we might as well take advantage of this boat and go on our honeymoon."

"I did what you wanted," Jamie said. "Why don't you just let them go?"

"They've seen too much. On our way to our honeymoon, we'll throw the bodies overboard. No one will think to look in the middle of the lake." He aimed his gun at the women.

He pulled the trigger just as Sam moved around the girls and fired back twice. Both struck Ernie in the left shoulder. He staggered and collapsed to the floor of the boat.

The gun skittered from Ernie's hand and into the girls' corner.

"Hands up, now!" the sheriff yelled from the dock.

No one knew quite how it happened. Somehow, Ernie managed to grab Alex by the hair. He held her in front of him for protection. With an eye of the sheriff, Ernie removed his knife from his sock and placed the knife at Alex's neck tight enough to cause a small amount of blood to trickle out.

"Shoot, and she's dead." Ernie was enjoying all the attention.

"Shoot him!" Alex yelled to the sheriff.

"Get your fucking hands in the air, sheriff!" he said and put more pressure on Alex's throat. Alex whimpered in pain. "The rest of you stay down on the ground."

He looked over his shoulder at Jared and Doug trying to noiselessly climb into the boat. "So glad you could make it," he said. "I've been waiting for you. On the ground with the sluts."

"He's going to kill us anyway!" Alex yelled.

"Keep your trap shut, you whore," Ernie said.

Doug lay on the deck face down. He saw Jamie was bleeding from her left arm. He knew he had to do something quick.

Doug caught Alex's eye while Ernie ranted and raved at the sheriff. With no time to think, Doug rolled sideways, grabbed a fishing pole, and whacked Ernie on the legs. Ernie dropped the knife and fell to his knees from the blow. Alex was pushed to ground by the force of Ernie. At first daze, Alex watched as Ernie slithered on his stomach toward a pile of fishing equipment. Alex saw the knife in front of her and grabbed it.

She tossed the knife to the sheriff. She didn't want it laying around for him to use as a weapon again. He was finding enough on his own.

Doug pulled out his gun and aimed it at Ernie.

"Stop! Put your hands where I can see them, now!" the sheriff ordered. He stood behind Doug with his weapon ready.

But Ernie stood up and faced them, the rifle in his hands.

"Sorry, sheriff. Drop the guns, gentleman."

Doug and the sheriff, outmatched, put down their weapons.

"It didn't have to be this way, Jamie," Ernie said. He aimed the rifle at Jamie.

Cristal grabbed Jamie, holding her tightly. Both girls closed their eyes.

Then Doug dropped low and rammed into Ernie. A rifle shot deafened him. Ernie landed on his back, and Doug held him down. Jared wrestled away the rifle.

Not ready to give in yet, Ernie did the only thing he could think of. As Doug landed on top of him, he sank his teeth into Doug's ear. Doug yelped in response. He reared back and hit Ernie dead on center in the nose. Red splattered on Ernie's face. He hit him in the face again, and then a third time. Finally, Doug forced himself to pull back even though he wanted to kill the bastard.

"Jamie, you know that we should've been together. It could've all worked out," he yelled.

Ernie continued to spit out obscenities as the sheriff handcuffed him and read him his rights. Jared quickly untied the priest from the chair and made sure he was unharmed.

Backup arrived just as they were hauling Ernie away from the group. Another team began the steps necessary to secure the area. The medical crew got to work. In the heat of everything, no one had noticed Jamie had been shot in the arm when the first shot was fired. Or that Cristal was shot in the leg—the rifle shot. Puddles of blood spilled out everywhere.

When Jared saw Cristal, he yelled for the paramedics to come immediately. Alex was bent over Cristal's side holding her hand tightly. It didn't look good. Blood was everywhere, spewing out of her lower leg at the bullet wound.

The medical team transferred her onto a gurney and rushed her to the hospital. Alex jumped in with her once she assured Jared and the medical team that she was okay and promised ten times to have a doctor look at her as soon as they arrived. Her neck was bleeding from where Ernie had pressed the knife, but she knew it look worse than it was. He had only cut the surface.

Doug, in the meantime, knelt by Jamie's side, her head in his lap. He sat rubbing her hair back. He was worried and trying not to show it. His stomach churned with anxiety. He knew Cristal's situation was more severe and needed immediate attention, but he was getting impatient.

Finally, they attended to Jamie, and moved everyone to the hospital. Alex, Doug, Jared, and the priest came out unscathed, but the sheriff insisted that everyone get examined. Apparently, Ernie had driven out of town the day before, stopped at the first church he came across, and kidnapped the priest.

Alex was out first with some antiseptic and a few bandages. They stitched up Jamie's arm and removed the bullet. She had lost a great deal of blood so they admitted her for monitoring. Other than that, she had some bumps and bruises. Nothing that wouldn't heal with time and rest.

Cristal had been rushed into surgery, and no one had heard anything. Jared, Sam, and Doug were trying their best to keep Alex calm.

"It's my fault," Alex said. "We should've waited for backup What were we thinking?"

"She came of her own free will," Jared said. "She's a grown woman, Alex."

Finally, after several hours, the doctor came to the waiting room to give an update.

"We're still operating. Cristal's lost a lot of blood. We removed the bullet. It did a lot of damage. The only way I think I can save her is to remove her lower left leg. I'm sorry," the doctor said.

Alex felt herself grow faint. Her legs buckled beneath her, and she held onto Jared for support.

"Will she live?" Alex asked.

"Her ligaments and tendons were severely damaged. Infection has set in. Everything should go well if we remove the leg."

Alex nodded.

*   *   *

Doug stood in the hallway for a few seconds before he entered Jamie's room. A pain squeezed at his heart seeing her there will those tubes in her, so vulnerable. It had been quite a weekend for him. He couldn't even begin to think what he'd have done if something had happened to her.

"Who's the handsome guy hiding behind the bouquet?" Jamie said.

"I didn't want to wake you."

"I'm awake. Come sit."

"How's the arm?"

"It's fine." Jamie paused. "How's Cristal?"

"Alex is with her now. She just woke up a few hours ago. She's going to be okay. They were able to save all of it but the lower ankle and foot. She will eventually be able to have a prosthetic."

"She probably needs those flowers more than I do."

"I already dropped her bouquet off. According to Alex, she prefers carnations. I ordered five dozen. One from each of us. I figured it's the least we could do," he said.

Jamie laughed at the thought of the little hospital room overflowing with flowers.

"What's going to happen to him, Doug?" Jamie said. A wave of apprehension swept through her.

"Don't worry, they're transporting him this morning to the city prison. He'll be there for the rest of his life on murder and kidnapping charges. Plus the other thirteen indictments he racked up. They denied his bail. He can't hurt you now."

"He took your ring, Doug," she said.

"The sheriff dropped this by this morning," he said. He opened the velvet box and took out the ring. "Let's try this again. Jamie, will you marry me?"

She smiled. "Yes. I will marry you."

Doug continued, "I know your job is everything. If it means us being together, Haley and I will move to Chicago if you'll have us. All that matters is that we're together. Wherever you are is where I want—"

"Wait, Doug," Jamie interrupted. "I know my career has been my life. I would've been lost not having it."

"It's part of who you are," Doug said.

She grabbed his hand. In her heart she'd always been afraid. Now it was time to lay it all on the line.

"It's part of who I was. I thought I was living. I was hiding. I can't go back even if I wanted to. I know what I'd be missing. You. Haley. This town. The group. I love you, and I will marry you. But, there's something I need to tell you first."

Doug looked at her with such love, it almost made her cry.

"I was pregnant after the rape. I never decided what to do because eight weeks later, I had a miscarriage. Since then I've had several surgeries for pre-cancerous cells. I may never be able to give you a family. I know that's important to you."

A flash of wild grief ripped through her as she waited for Doug's response.

Doug reached out and held her tight. "That doesn't matter to me. You are my family, you and Haley. If we don't have any other children, that's fine with me. And there's time for all that. Besides, you have a wedding to plan."

"Yes, I do, and I can't wait," Jamie said, her joy coursing through her.

"We can plan the weddings on weekends when we see each other."

"No, I don't think so," Jamie said. "I want to be here, in my hometown with you. Life's too short to spend it working all the time."

"Are you sure?"

"I'm sure. I just need to wrap up a few things with work and my condo, give notice, and move everything home. Let's go six weeks for the wedding just to be sure Cristal is able to be there. Haley could be a bridesmaid or the flower girl."

"You called it home," Doug said, grinning.

"Get used to it."

Jamie held back the tears thinking of her homemade card she tediously prepared ten years ago. Funny how some things just work out.

"I hope we're not interrupting anything," Sam said as she and Alex peaked their heads in for a visit.

"We can always come back later," Alex said.

"Don't be silly. Come in."

"I'll give you girls some time and check in on Cristal," Doug said and left.

"How are you feeling?" Sam asked.

"I'm fine, actually more than fine. Do you think you guys could help plan a wedding in six weeks?" Jamie held out her hand to show off her new ring.

"Congratulations!" Alex said and hugged her best friend.

"Who's the lucky guy?" Sam joked.

"Very funny."

"I would be honored if both of you, and Cristal of course, would serve as my bridesmaids."

Both girls screamed in excitement, jumping up and down.

"I'll warn you, though, it's going to be quite a job. First assignment: go to the gift shop and bring me bridal magazines."

"Second assignment: schedule a bachelorette party," Sam said, excited by the idea.

CHAPTER 19

Jared, dressed in a black tux, escorted Jamie down the aisle to give her away to his best friend. As all eyes were upon her, she almost had to pinch herself to make sure it was real. The whole event reminded her of the storybooks she had read when she was a child. The prince, princess, and happily ever after.

Both her mother and grandmother had left her their wedding dresses. The dresses were old and in need of repair, but each dress had good material here and there. With a little shopping and lots of creativity, Alex was able to use both dresses to make the gown of Jamie's dreams. One she would remember forever. It was a wonderful combination of silk and satin with spaghetti straps and a long train. She wanted something different for her wedding, so that no memory of her forced one would interfere. Thankfully, those vows did not stand under forced pretenses. She had also chosen no veil for the same reason and decided to let her hair hang freely in loose curls.

The dress covered the something old. Doug's mom lent her a gorgeous sapphire and diamond bracelet, which took care of the borrowed and blue. Alex, Sam, Cristal, and Jared bought her an exquisite pair of diamond stud earrings for the something new. The girls chose navy blue floor-length gowns for the bridesmaid's attire. Alex had just enough material left to construct a miniature version of her dress for Haley, a surprise for Doug. Haley would be walking down the aisle directly behind her, and also had her hair flowing in soft curls to mimic Jamie's.

After much debate, the farm was chosen for both the wedding and reception. As Jamie stood waiting for the organist to begin playing, she glanced around the packed assembly. The community had once again joined forces to make this dream a reality. A little flower shop volunteered to handle all the arrangements. Various displays of roses overpowered the room with bright colors. The local women's chapter insisted on handling the food. Doug's mom prepared the cake, a three-tiered chocolate cake topped with a Precious Moments groom and bride. Jamie frantically worked all week ordering and setting up tents, tables, and chairs. Jared had even talked the football team into helping him make a wooden awning where they could say their vows. For one day, the farm had been transformed into her own little wonderland. Jamie was so proud the way everyone had worked to make it happen.

The organist began as Jamie and Haley took long strides down the aisle. Doug exhaled a long sigh of contentment and literally had to gasp for air as he saw the two most beautiful girls coming towards him down the aisle. His heart sang with delight as the pastor began the ceremony.

"Jamie, it's my understanding you have written some words you would like to share?"

"I do, yes," she said as she reached out for Doug's hand. She looked into his eyes. "My journey in life has led me both to and away from you. I stand before you today and look into your eyes, and I know without a doubt, I'm finally where I'm supposed to be.

This is my home here with you. Douglas Michael Miller. am honored to become your wife, to have and to hold through sickness and health. I love your passion for family, your sense of humor, your trust and honesty, and most of all, your never-ending faith and belief in me. I give you my promise here today, I will always love both you and Haley for all my days. I will support and stand by you as my husband." Tears crept from the corner of her eyes.

"Do you, Jamie Lyn Donald, take this man to be your husband?" the pastor asked.

"I do," she said, feeling a bottomless peace and satisfaction.

"Doug, would you like to say anything?" the pastor asked.

"You are my soul mate, my first and last love. I was lucky enough to find you in the beginning. Yet dumb enough to let you go. Without you, I was empty. Now, I'm filled with life again. You brought back the joy. I will never take your for granted. I'm proud to be your husband."

"You may kiss the bride," the pastor said.

Doug reached over and planted a soft, meaningful kiss onto Jamie's lips. The first one as husband and wife.

Everyone cheered and threw birdseed as they ran hand-in-hand down the aisle. Jamie felt a warm glow flow through her on this special day as she looked around at all the loved ones who joined her. Sam, Alex, Cristal, and Haley agreed to stand up with her. Cristal's recovery was going well, and she was using a wheelchair temporarily. Over a hundred friends and family came to celebrate their day of joy. The sun was out, the birds chirping, and she was now Mrs. Doug Miller. She was finally home.

"Jamie, I'd like to ask you something," Alex said.

"Sure, go ahead."

"If it's okay with you, I'd like the first picture to be one with all of us in it. Our new family. Only if you don't mind," Alex said.

"I think that's a wonderful idea," Jamie responded. She was blissfully happy and fully alive.

"Here in the garden would be a perfect place. I'll get Doug and Haley if you want to gather your brother, Sam, and Cristal," Jamie said.

"It seems like the best way to start our new life together as a family," Alex said.

As the photographer snapped his pictures Jamie knew this was the best day of her life. Joy bubbled in her smile and shone in her eyes. A new beginning with her new family.

EPILOGUE

"Now that you're married, we have a favor to ask you," Alex said, standing with Sam.

"Sure, what is it?" Jamie asked.

"Meet us tomorrow morning, 7 a.m. at this address. I know you're leaving in the afternoon for Hawaii. So we'll keep it short, but it's important," Alex said.

"What's going on here? You guys have that look on your faces," Jamie asked.

"Just trust us, 7 a.m., here's the address," Sam said, handing her a piece of paper.

The next day, Jamie got up early and drove to the address on the paper. The secrecy of it had kept her up most of the night. She tried to get information out of Doug, but if he knew anything, he wasn't talking. It was probably an after-wedding gift.

She pulled up to the address and parked along the street curb. She saw all three girls giddy and full of smiles in front of a vacant building. She definitely knew something was going on now because with the exception of Alex, none of them were morning people.

"What do you think?" they chorused together.

"What do I think about what? Have you guys started doing drugs?" she asked.

"We decided to open our own business, a secondhand décor store. But we need a marketing and business partner," Sam said.

"Selling junk? You want me to sell junk? I don't know anything about stores," Jamie said.

"It's not junk. One person's garbage is another person's treasure. We would only carry fine quality items. And, you don't need to know anything; I know enough for all of us. We need someone who knows about marketing and business management," Alex said

"That I know," Jamie said. She couldn't believe she was actually considering the insane idea.

"Since you're unemployed and all, we figured you can't be too picky," Sam said.

"Since I'm here, let's go take a look," Jamie said. "Spacious room, decent area, easy access, good parking, it could work. Of course, we'd have to put a budget together. A marketing profile, a profit and loss worksheet, make a list of supplies, contact…" she paused when she saw that everyone was laughing at her. "What's so funny?"

"That's exactly why we need you. We would never think of all that. We just want to work with customers and sell second-hand treasures," Alex said.

"I know what works. How to make a lot with a little. To find the value in what others might just trash," Alex said with such passion Jamie couldn't have said no, even if she wanted to. Before she could say anything, Sam threw her pitch to convince Jamie.

"I love the customer end of it. I know I could work a sales floor like no one else."

"What do you say, partners?" Alex asked.

"What exactly would we sell again?" Jamie asked, still pondering the opportunity.

"House decorations, small appliances, interior supplies, crafts, antiques, books, and other household items. We should do well with the local college in town," Alex responded.

"What would we call it, 'Junk Is Us?'" Jamie asked.

"Very funny. For your information, missy, we will only carry items and antiques in excellent condition," Alex said.

"Second Chances," Sam said.

"What?" Jamie asked.

"'Second Chances' would be the name. To represent the items in the store and the three of us with our second chance together with our lives," Sam said.

"A shop owner," Jamie said. "Who would've guessed."

"Is that a yes?" Sam said.

"How could I say no to that sales pitch?" She laughed. "Yes. That's a yes. Why not? Of course, I need to review the lease first, and do a quick analysis to make sure there's a decent profit ratio. While I'm gone, you'll need to fix this place up a bit and add a fresh coat of paint. I'll make a list, and then there's inventory." She stopped when she realized they were staring at her and rolling their eyes. "Sorry, second nature."

"Are you part of this conspiracy?" Jamie asked Cristal, noticing she'd been quiet through their pitch.

"I have enough work on the farm. I'm just along for support and to offer my services as a part-time employee. This is your guys' deal," Cristal said.

"We'll keep you busy," Alex said. "To think the four of us, a team, how exciting!"

Then Sam brought out a small bag she had been hiding. In it were four plastic champagne glasses and a bottle of champagne. She popped the top and poured everyone a drink.

"I'd like to propose a toast. To good friends, great towns, and second chances."

They all raised their glasses.

"To second chances," they cheered.

THE END

Made in the USA
Monee, IL
18 January 2023

25448249R00132